FIREBALL

FIREBALL

by John Christopher

E. P. DUTTON   NEW YORK

Copyright © 1981 by John Christopher

Library of Congress Cataloging in Publication Data

Christopher, John.   Fireball.

Summary: Two boys are drawn by a fireball into a
society, parallel to twentieth-century England, which
has many of the characteristics of Roman Britain.
[1. Space and time—Fiction]   I. Title.
PZ7.C457Fi   1981   [Fic]   80-22094   ISBN: 0-525-29738-3

Published in the United States by Elsevier-Dutton
Publishing Co., Inc., 2 Park Avenue, New York, N.Y. 10016

Published simultaneously in Canada by Clarke,
Irwin & Company Limited, Toronto and Vancouver

Editor: Ann Durell   Designer: Claire Counihan

Printed in the U.S.A.   First Edition

10 9 8 7 6 5 4 3 2 1

To Ann
in gratitude for aid and encouragement
and superb editing

Simon and his American cousin Brad
hadn't wanted to spend the summer
together. And the quiet London suburb
where Simon lived was the last place
they expected anything unusual to
happen.

Then the fireball came. The huge
whirling ball of light was like nothing
the boys had ever seen before—and they
felt compelled to investigate.

They awoke in a world where everything had changed. It was still England,
but an England terrifyingly different
from the one they had suddenly left
behind.

They had passed through the fireball. And they would have to learn to
survive in the fascinatingly strange
world on the other side.

I

THE GRANNIES, sitting drinking tea in the dining room, were talking about the old days, in the war. Simon caught a snatch of their conversation: ". . . the time we went to that dance and then had to spend all night in the air-raid shelter in the Broadway . . ." That was Yankee Granny, which was the obvious way of distinguishing her from his own granny. He heard a ripple of laughter. "I never could *stand* him." Granny, this time. It was all right for them, he supposed. They had plenty to talk about, the past to ransack.

He gazed, without much favour, at the chessboard in front of him. He had been playing chess for two or three years, and when Brad admitted becoming acquainted with the game only the previous winter, it had seemed a promising opportunity for putting Brad down. Things had started well, too, with Simon getting the better of the

1

early exchanges. Since then, though, the position had altered; he not only had fewer pieces left, but Brad's forces were ominously well placed to attack.

There had been a lot of what he now saw as propaganda heralding this visit. The impression had almost been given that it had been planned for his benefit, rather than as a reunion for the two grannies and an opportunity for Brad's mother to holiday in Europe with his new stepfather. It was going to be fascinating for him, having his American cousin for a couple of weeks in the summer. (Cousin once removed, his father had pointed out—his mother and Brad's mother were the actual cousins—but that didn't make it any less interesting, of course.) A broadening experience, and fun at the same time. And now that the families had become reacquainted, there were lots of other possibilities. A return visit by him to Vermont the following year, perhaps?

Looking at the board again, Simon saw a possibility he had not previously noticed. Knight to queen's five. It offered a threat to Brad's queen, and when he moved the queen, it would leave a pawn unguarded and also open a route by which Simon's queen could advance on the other flank. He made the move.

Despite the propaganda, he had not been keen on the idea. In the first place, half his form at school, including his best friend Grendall, were down for the school's cruise to Greece, and he'd assumed he would be going, too. In the second, it meant sharing a room, and after ten weeks in a school dormitory he didn't want to share a room with anyone. Not even Grendall, much less some American who most likely talked noisily all the time.

He had pressed his objections with Granny and his

mother and thought he might be getting somewhere. By a fortunate coincidence the dates of the projected visit coincided almost exactly with the cruise dates. And the notice about the cruise had arrived at half-term, before the American invasion had been broached even. As far as the Americans were concerned, that could already have been fixed, so there was no question of his seeming discourteous or unwelcoming. It offered the advantage, in fact, that Cousin Brad (once removed) could have a room to himself.

But when he carried the campaign to his father, his hopes were promptly and firmly dashed. There was, it appeared, no question of his going on the cruise in any case. Times were hard, and the extra expense just could not be managed. It was going to be difficult enough coping with the latest increase in school fees, news of which had arrived that morning. There was a look in his father's eye which Simon recognized, and he did not attempt to argue.

Instead, with no alternative in view, he did his best to look on the bright side of the impending visit. By the time it actually occurred, two weeks after the end of the summer term, he had had time to get bored with his own company and was even, warily, looking forward to it.

The first couple of days were confusing because apart from Brad there were his mother and stepfather (sleeping in a hotel nearby, but filling the house by day) and his grandmother. But Simon's first impressions were favourable. Brad was smaller than he was, shorter and wirier, with fair hair and blue eyes and a cheerful grin. He looked, Simon reflected, more English than he himself, with his large-boned swarthiness and brown eyes, did. Moreover, he wasn't as extrovert and noisy as one expected an American to be. In fact, he tended to leave Simon to make the running conversationally, though that could have been due to shyness. Except that shyness would be non-American, too, wouldn't it?

Simon dutifully did his best to bring his cousin out. It wasn't too easy. He asked about American football, to be told Brad wasn't much interested in football. He moved on to baseball, reminding himself not to make any comparison with rounders, or mention the word for that matter. Brad disclaimed any interest in baseball either. Simon asked if he played *any* sports, preparing to take the generous view that not everyone did, and it was really no defect not to.

"Well, skiing," Brad told him. "And tennis and golf and surfing. And windsurfing."

That was when Simon felt the first prickle of unease, verging on hostility.

Brad's parents departed on their extended tour—London, Paris, Switzerland, Rome, and finally Yugoslavia, where Brad's stepfather had family ties of his own to renew. It sounded like fun. More fun than his own exercise (or chore) in cementing transatlantic relations, but he applied himself to the task with resolution, if not enthusiasm. The two grannies, reminiscing about the blitz or Mafeking or Sebastopol or whatever, got on like a couple of houses on fire, completely failing to notice that at a junior level any sparking was of quite a different order.

What bugged Simon was that while he had been prepared to make allowances, lend a helping hand and all that, he found no taker for his generosity. And while he had been determined not to say or do anything which might make his American cousin feel inferior or embarrassed, it was more than slightly galling to have evidence of the other's superiority thrust down his throat instead. The day after Brad's parents left he overheard Yankee Granny telling her sister about Brad: His IQ was 150, he had an incredible photographic memory so that he could recite whole pages out of an encyclopaedia, and it wasn't a . . . you know . . . *narrow* talent. Brad had such wide interests. She'd read an article in *Reader's Digest* about the Renaissance Man—taking all of knowledge as his province, you know? That was the way Brad was.

Simon's grandmother had come back bravely with her own grandchild boast, but she had, Simon recognized, been outgunned; or, to put it more accurately, had been short of similar calibre ammunition. Animosity began crystallizing into a fairly hearty dislike.

The simple fact remained, though, that he was stuck with the situation—and Brad—for another three weeks. He continued putting on as good a show of amiability as possible. When he told Brad the joke about the Red Indian and the eggs, the *aim* had been to make him feel at home. (He had mentally censored the one about Custer's Last Stand as possibly offensive to the Spirit of American History.)

The joke, though, did not provoke amusement. Instead, he was treated to a lecture on the American Indian and the wickedness of his exploitation by Europeans. Brad clearly knew a lot about American Indians and their history, and under other circumstances Simon might have found it interesting. But smarting over the failure of his attempt at humour, and the implied charges of both ignorance and racial guilt—Brad presumably being absolved through knowing all that and being pro-Indian—he felt more like choking the lecturer.

There was another clash at the weekend, this time involving his parents. The television news had been on, showing yet another scene of mob violence somewhere, and he had quoted the bit about Napoleon sorting out the Paris mob with a whiff of grapeshot. Brad said that was the sort of idea Hitler had, too, and somehow Simon found himself arguing not just with Brad but with his parents as well. He felt, moreover, that he had been manoeuvred into defending a view he really didn't hold, but was not prepared to shift sides. He went to bed seething, and turned a glowering back on Brad's good-night from the other side of the room.

Coming back to chess, Simon realized Brad had spent a longer time than usual considering the position; his earlier moves had been made very quickly, another source of irritation. Simon studied the board himself, with satisfaction. When Brad moved his queen, it offered more than just an attacking position. There was a mate in three—he could see it clearly.

Brad leaned forward, hesitated, then moved not his queen, but one of his castles. His hand hovered above the piece, then lifted. Simon, after another quick look to make sure none of his own pieces was at risk, moved his knight and whipped off Brad's queen before he had time to try changing his mind. He sat back, feeling pleased.

Brad said: "Castle to knight's eight. Followed by knight to bishop's five. Check and mate, whatever you do."

Simon stared at the arena of black and white squares, seeking for a way out. How had he managed to overlook that knight? He mentally booted himself and thought longingly of doing the same physically to Brad. It was mate all right. No possible doubt.

Brad said: "I was sure you'd spot it. That's why I did

that misdirection—hesitating before I moved, and after. I'm sorry about that. Nothing in the rules against it, but I guess it's not entirely fair."

Especially, Simon thought, when you reckon you're playing against a cretin. He gathered up the pieces in silence. His chess instructor in school had made it a drill that you congratulated your opponent when you lost a game, but the words stuck in his throat.

He had been half aware of a lull in the talk next door. Granny now looked in on them. Brad said: "You feel like another game?"

"How are you two?" Granny asked.

"Fine."

He wanted another game the way he wanted a broken leg, but to admit that would be giving Brad best again. Before he could say anything, though, Granny said: "You really ought not to be stuck indoors, on an afternoon like this. Why don't you take Tarka out on a badger hunt?"

Simon glanced at Brad, who nodded politely.

"Sure, Mrs Roberts," Brad said.

Better to take Tarka for a walk than endure another game of chess. It meant having Brad along, but he was stuck with that anyway. He said: "If you like, Granny. Do you know where her lead is?"

The house was on the outskirts of the suburb, only a few hundred yards from open country. They headed that way in silence. The morning had been misty, but it was hot now—oppressively so. The present heat wave had lasted a week and was about due to break. The air was heavy, and though the sky overhead was blue, thunderclouds towered on the horizon.

7

The road ended with Saxmundham Villas, giving way to fields. Simon kept Tarka on her lead while they crossed them; there were cattle, and although she was only a miniature dachshund, she had a disproportionately large streak of aggression in her makeup. He wondered what point the cruise ship had reached. One of the smaller Greek islands? Wherever it was, distinctly preferable to an outer London suburb and the company of Brad and Tarka. They crossed the third field and went through a gate into open wooded country, rising ground. Simon released the dog and watched her gallop uphill on her ludicrous little legs, her nose sweeping the grass like a Hoover.

He supposed he ought to say something to Brad.

"There aren't any badgers here, as far as we know. It's sort of Granny's joke."

"Sure. Dachshund. Means badger hound. They raised them for badger baiting, in Germany."

Obviously, Simon thought, it was too much to ask that just once Brad could be told something, instead of knowing it in advance. Thunder rumbled angrily, seeming much closer than the clouds would have led one to think. He felt hot and sticky, and as irrationally angry as the thunder sounded.

He said, with heavy sarcasm: "That makes them a bad breed of dog, I suppose?"

"Bad?"

"Being German."

It annoyed him further when Brad at once picked up the reference to the argument on Sunday. "We were talking about Hitler."

"I like the Germans," Simon said. "They've got some

idea of order and discipline. They're not weak and sloppy, like some countries."

"Something in that. We've still had to fight them twice in this century."

"We?"

He put a lot into that monosyllable. He stared at Brad and got a stare back; negative, bland almost. Brad said: "As I recall, the Germans surrendered to Field Marshal Montgomery in 1945 at Lüneburg Heath. As I also recall, he was serving at the time under a guy called Eisenhower."

Simon said: "Our school caretaker fought alongside the Americans in North Africa. He was in the Guards. He said they always used to say the next war would be between the two yellow nations—the Chinese and the Americans."

There was another rumble of thunder, seeming almost directly behind Brad. They stood facing each other. A smile was starting on Brad's face, and Simon had mixed thoughts. He already regretted the remark, but the fact of Brad's swallowing the insult undoubtedly made up for quite a lot.

He didn't have time to banish the satisfaction or clear his thoughts before he found himself flat on his back in the rough grass. Brad had pulled the punch out of nowhere and delivered it fast. It had been heavier than he would have expected, too, but it was being off-balance that had felled him. He got to his feet, while Brad watched him expressionlessly.

"Right," Simon said.

It was soon apparent that, although he had not mentioned it, boxing was also a sport in which Brad had had more than a little practice. He took up a proper stance, though southpaw, and used his fists scientifically. He was fast, too, and at the beginning landed more punches, particularly stinging raps to the face. What he lacked, of course, was weight.

They exchanged punches, circling and stumbling on the uneven ground. Simon had a glimpse of Tarka watching them earnestly from a few feet away, and the distraction earned him a jolting blow to the ribs. He was concentrating on body blows himself; Brad's guard was weaker there. He dropped Brad, waited for him to get up, and then put him down a second time. As Brad got once more to his feet, Simon suddenly felt ashamed. His opponent was at least three inches shorter and maybe twenty pounds lighter. He stepped back, as Brad squared up.

"OK, I'm sorry," Simon said. Brad watched him warily. "It was a stupid thing to say."

Brad gave him a long considering look, then nodded slowly and grinned. He put a hand forward, and Simon took it. They shook. Brad said: "I was only going to point out you were bleeding. . . . Did you know that? But fine, anyway."

Simon became aware of a trickle of blood on his right cheek. He wiped it with the arm of his shirt.

"Better?"

"Yes. It's only a nick." Brad came closer and examined it. "You won't need surgery, but it's something they'll notice."

"I ran into a branch. Or got snagged on a bramble."

"Something like that." Brad grinned again. "I guess we should have done this a few days ago."

Tarka was staring up at them. Simon whistled cheerfully to her.

"Come on, you miserable little bitch. Let's find those badgers."

They continued the walk in companionable conversation. Brad, it emerged, had been at least as reluctant over the trip as Simon. He had wanted to travel west, not east. His father, who had also remarried, lived in California.

"On the coast, north of Los Angeles. And I really mean *on* the coast. His house is right on the beach, and you ought to see the breakers. Fantastic surfing."

Surfing was an unknown world to Simon, but the regret in Brad's voice carried conviction. He said: "Your mother wouldn't let you go?"

"Oh, she'd let me all right. She has to share me, half and half, for the summer vacation, with Dad calling the shots over when."

"So why not?"

"Because she and Hank just got married. She's worried that I won't get along with him. I like him well enough, but short of sending him roses I don't know how I'm going to convince her."

"But if your father calls the shots . . ."

"Hank was determined they should go on this trip to Europe. She'd have been miserable if I'd stayed behind."

"You've stayed behind here."

"I meant, stay behind and visit L.A. She doesn't mind leaving me here."

"But she needed to have your father agree?"

"I wrote him and asked. He's a pretty reasonable guy."

"Yes."

There was a silence, no longer unfriendly. Cloud had built fast, hiding the sun. The ground, as they walked

11

uphill, had become more wooded, until they were following a path with trees and bushes close on either side. Tarka galloped ahead, stopping occasionally to savour some specially pungent patch of ground.

Brad said: "You had plans, too?"

Simon told him about the cruise. Brad nodded sympathetically. "Tough."

"Yes, but . . ."

He stopped as Tarka, cravenly yelping, bolted down the path, towards and past them. He turned, calling her, but she continued at full pelt. He was about to give chase when Brad spoke.

"Look at that. . . ."

Simon caught the note of incredulity and turned back. Brad was pointing, but the gesture was unnecessary. It was coming slowly towards them from the spot at which Tarka had taken fright. He felt his hair prickle.

"What is it?"

Brad didn't answer. It was roughly spherical, eight or ten feet across, blindingly white—a whiteness of sunlight reflected dazzlingly from mist or ice. Except that there was no sun. It appeared to float a foot or so above the ground. Thunder growled, and a heavy drop of rain splashed Simon's face. He said: "It's what they call a fireball, isn't it? I've read about them."

The progress had slowed and now halted. It hovered a dozen feet away from them. That was some relief, but he still didn't like the look of it. He was trying to reassure himself by adding: "A form of ball lightning. Quite harmless."

Brad said slowly: "I guess it has to be ball lightning. Only ball lightning's supposed to be coloured—red or yellow. And nothing so big—no more than inches across."

He took a step forward.

Simon, alarmed, said: "I'd watch it. Even if it is supposed to be harmless, I wouldn't try interfering with it."

"Whatever it is," Brad said, "I doubt we'll ever see anything like it again. I want to see it close up."

The huge ball did not move, but Simon's hairs still prickled. It could be static electricity causing that, but it could also be the same old-fashioned cowardice which had sent Tarka streaking for home.

Brad continued advancing. For Simon, the thought of Tarka produced the attractive thought that he was responsible for her and maybe ought to go after her and make sure she was all right. The prospect of explaining that to Brad later was something he liked rather less. Or he could just stand his ground, while Brad went forward and investigated. And then listen to Brad's report on it?

He made a conscious, sweating effort to move his feet, and followed Brad. The fireball stayed on the same spot, but he had a feeling, as much from intuition as from anything he could actually see, that it was spinning on its axis. And somehow inside the dazzling white there seemed to be colours—hundreds and thousands of tiny winking jewels. He said uneasily: "It's quite pretty."

He wasn't sure what happened next—whether the sphere moved like a lightning stroke towards them, or suddenly expanded. There was a weird sensation of rapid motion and absolute stillness at the same time and a quivering in his body as though every joint and every muscle were being violently twitched. He thought, with detachment: So this is what it's like being electrocuted. Then all the white was black.

II

IT WAS LIKE AWAKENING from sleep by being tossed into a cold bath. The sensation of stinging wetness was so vivid that Simon put a hand to his face and was surprised to find both dry. There had been a moment of unconsciousness, but it seemed no more than a moment, with the recollection of what had happened immediately before it intense and real. As real as the present awareness of lying on the ground, where he must have fallen.

The fireball? There was no sign of it. He looked around him into an ordinary wood on an ordinary hot grey afternoon. Brad? Yes, Brad was there behind him, getting to his feet. Simon stood up, too. His muscles trembled slightly but obeyed him. He turned round to look properly at Brad, a deliberate act. No, there was nothing wrong with him. He lifted his right arm, clenching the fist

14

tight. As far as he could tell, anyway. He asked tentatively: "Brad?"

"Yes."

"What happened?"

"I'm not sure. The ball hit us, I guess. You OK?"

"Yes. You?"

Brad nodded. "It must be true they're harmless. Or maybe we just lucked out. Static electricity does funny things."

Simon remembered the first intimation of something out of place: the dog's panic flight. Turning to look in the direction she'd gone, he was aware of another jolt, but mental, not physical. There was no path. He was standing on unmarked, rough ground in the middle of the wood. But where in the wood? That vast spreading tree, its gnarled trunk several feet across, had not been there. He would have noticed it. Trying to keep the nervousness out of his voice, he said: "Where are we?"

"That's what I was starting to wonder." Brad reached up to an overhanging branch and shook it, as though testing its reality. "Not where we were when we got hit."

"That's crazy!" He hesitated. "Some sort of dream?"

Brad let go of the branch. He came towards Simon and, before Simon realized what was happening, had given him a short punch, jolting rather than painful, to the ribs. He grinned.

"That feel like a dream?"

"But what . . . ?"

"Maybe a freak atmospheric condition. You read about those rains of frogs from the sky? We got picked up and then dumped. In another part of the wood."

Simon looked up at the sky. "No wind then. Or now."

15

"But in between? I was out. Not long, I guess, but how would I know? And you?"

"Yes, but . . ."

"Long enough, maybe, for some kind of updraft to lift us."

"And set us down again, both in the same spot, without a bruise?"

Brad shrugged. "You have a better explanation?"

"It would make as much sense to have been taken—I don't know—to another planet or something."

"Not to me, it wouldn't." Brad was emphatic. "A planet with an atmosphere as near the same as ours as makes no difference? And flora. That's a good old-fashioned oak tree." He pointed. "Complete with squirrel."

It was sound reasoning, but did not affect the feeling of total strangeness, of dislocation from reality, which had been growing rather than diminishing since he picked himself up. Simon looked about him. A normal sky, an ordinary wood. The squirrel had halted on an upper branch of the oak and was brushing whiskers with paws. Well, one would be strange, dislocated, after getting knocked out by some weird electrical thing and physically shifted around by an even weirder typhoon. He said: "I suppose we might as well try getting back."

"Yes. Back where, though? We don't have any idea whereabouts in the wood we are. Do you know?"

"No. But the wood's not large. And once we're out of it, I'll know where I am. Even if we come out on the far side."

Brad nodded. "I guess that figures. So lead on. You're the trailblazer."

They had originally been walking uphill, so Simon set

off down; the wood covered the crest of a hill, so down had to be right, like following water. It wasn't particularly easy going. There were places where they had to struggle through undergrowth, or skirt it. Altogether the wood was far denser than he recalled, but he didn't know the southern part very well. And they seemed to have been travelling longer than he would have expected without coming to open country. Brad commented on that eventually.

"Could we be circling, do you think?"

It was not offered critically, but it annoyed him. He said shortly: "No."

"A small wood, you said."

"It's deceptive. Save your breath."

Brad obediently stayed silent, but Simon was starting to worry again. They should have been clear of the trees by now, in whichever direction they were heading. He pressed on faster, with Brad slogging after him. Were the trees thinner over on the left, and was that a glimpse of open sky? He headed that way. Definitely thinner, and more sky. They pushed through the last few feet and stood in the open, the wood behind them, grassland in front. Sheep grazed in the distance.

The only trouble was, he hadn't the faintest notion where they were. The wood, he knew, was surrounded on three sides by built-up areas, with open country to the south. But the lie of the land was wrong for the southern outskirts, and for that matter where were Ruckton church and the village?

"Anywhere you know?" Brad asked.

An innocent question, but he resented it. He stared about him without answering. Brad went on: "If it moved us from one part of the wood to another, I suppose it

17

could just as well have taken us further. To another wood. Another country even. You think those sheep could be Australian?"

"That's ridiculous."

"I know. But I'm starting not to be able to tell the ridiculous from the normal." Brad drew a deep breath. "Well, wherever we are, I guess we might as well keep moving. We're bound to get to some place with people if we walk far enough."

There was more woodland on the far side of the open land, ahead and to the left, but only occasional clumps of trees to the right. Brad set off that way, and after a brief hesitation Simon followed him. They approached sheep, which first stared at them and then moved away. They seemed to be on the small side, but had quite large black horns. The ground continued to open out. They were coming down into a valley, and he saw the distant gleam of a river. Something tugged at his memory and then was lost.

"Head for the river," Brad said.

"Why?"

"Why not?"

What he had really meant, Simon realized, was why do as you say? What gives you the right to make the decisions? He was only a stranger in this country. Providing, of course, this was England. He looked all around again and saw them, about a quarter of a mile back but heading this way. Horsemen—five or six.

He took Brad's arm and gestured. Brad said with relief: "Great! People. They can tell us where we are and the right road to somewhere."

They were oddly dressed, Simon noticed. It was difficult to pick out the details of clothing at this distance, but it didn't look right. Not the casual hacking gear you would expect to see in the Home Counties, certainly. Some kind of cloaks?

He said: "As long as we can be sure the natives are friendly. Can we?"

Brad paused. "I get you. Might be an idea to duck back among the trees and watch this bunch go past?"

They started moving quietly uphill. There was a rise of ground which would soon cut them off from the view of the horsemen, provided they had not already been spotted. Then there was a cry, unintelligible but sounding peremptory. Simon looked back as they automatically quickened step. The horsemen had changed direction to follow them. And they had urged their animals into a canter.

Brad had seen it, too. He said: "Run for it! Into the wood . . ."

Simon did not need telling. He pounded uphill, ahead of Brad. He could hear cries from their pursuers and felt the beat of hooves on the ground. The edge of the wood was about fifty yards away—a long fifty yards with the horsemen closing in.

Brad was falling behind. Simon thought about slowing to let him catch up, but fear kept him running hard; another glance back had shown an arm raised and a glint of what looked horribly like a sword. Then he heard a grunt and looked round to see Brad trip and fall heavily.

Simon was almost at the trees, and the horsemen were near enough for him to hear the panting of the horses as well as the shouts of the riders. He ran on, and branches whipped his face. He pushed through bushes and heard a clamour behind him. But the din lessened bit by bit as he struggled on through the undergrowth. When at last he leaned, gasping, against the trunk of a tree to get his breath back, he could hear no other sound apart from birds.

Simon gave it a long time, at least half an hour, before he started cautiously picking his way back through the wood, and he frequently stopped to listen. The final dozen or so yards to the point where the trees ended he took very warily indeed. When he poked his head out at last, it was in the half expectation of hearing a triumphant cry and seeing a menacing figure in front of him. There was nothing but the empty slope, grazing sheep, the river in the distance. No horsemen, and no Brad.

He sat down on the grass and thought about that. He couldn't possibly have saved him. If he had stopped and turned back . . . by the time he had reached Brad the horsemen would have been on top of both of them. What help would it have been to Brad for him to be caught as well? There was no flaw in the argument. All the same, going over it again didn't make him feel any better.

What had happened to Brad anyway? They hadn't killed him, or if they had, they must have taken the body with them. Actually the place where he had entered the wood, where Brad had fallen, was a bit further up the slope. He got to his feet and went there, examining the ground closely. No sign of blood. Perhaps the horsemen had been friendly; perhaps he'd been a fool to run away. He remembered the glint of steel; they hadn't looked friendly. And if they'd merely stopped to pass the time of day and tell Brad the way to the nearest railway station, Brad would have come into the wood and called him.

For that matter, where *were* they? Brad's notion of their having been transported by some atmospheric freak seemed less and less reasonable. Horsemen waving swords on the fringes of Greater London—or anywhere in Great Britain . . . unless they had dropped in a spot where a film or TV company was on location, it was crazy. And there was no sign of cameras or a film crew. Not Britain, then. Not Europe or America, either. Somewhere remote, like Afghanistan? But how, and why?

It had to be the fireball that had caused it. Not by picking them up and putting them down, like a playful typhoon, but in some quite different way. A gateway? Could they have passed through it and come out in a different place? But a place where you got run down by barbarous-looking horsemen with swords. Place—or *time*? A gateway to the past. Or maybe to the future, and a new Dark Age after the world had blown itself up as thoroughly as some people had suggested it might.

Simon shook his head, unhappy and bewildered. Compared with either of those, the notion of being transported across just a few thousand miles to Afghanistan seemed both more likely and overwhelmingly attractive. He looked down to the valley. Time had been passing while all this was going on. It was getting towards evening; the sun, though obscured by thick cloud, must be well down in the sky. Dusk and then night were not far off, and there must be a better place than this in which to face them.

He set off in the direction Brad had chosen earlier—towards the river. He slogged on, becoming aware as he did so of the growing pangs of hunger. Lunch was a long time back—or a thousand years in the future? He closed his mind to that and walked faster.

The river was further away than he had imagined, but

he reached it at last. This was a river untouched by man, swirling and gurgling and lapping against marshy banks. A trout rose to take a late fly under a rapidly darkening sky. Which way? When in doubt, downstream. Not that he felt it was likely to make any difference. He was tired and hungry, and very depressed.

Dusk thickened. It would be night soon, a night without yellow windows or streetlamps or even the cold beams of car headlights. Without paved roads and sidewalks, too. He slipped in a patch of mud and recovered himself on one knee. The river, almost invisible, had a melancholy, unfriendly sound.

He had almost gone past before he saw it—a squat, low building on his right. He hesitated only briefly before turning away from the river to investigate. His fingers found stone, and then a flat roof, within his reach. Not a house, not big enough for a stable even. But there was a kind of window: unglassed, an aperture only. Simon peered inside. A light flickered, a candle he thought at first, then saw it was a primitive form of oil lamp. It stood on a stone slab, and other things stood beside it: rough pottery plates bearing a round loaf, slices of meat, fruit.

Hunger overcame caution. He whispered: "Anyone there?" No reply, no sound at all from the shadows inside. His stomach growled at him. If he reached in, past the lamp, he could grab the loaf. He had almost done that when his arm brushed the lamp. It skittered off the slab, crashed to the stone floor, and went out.

Simon stood still, his heart pounding. If there had been anybody inside, that would have roused him. Nothing happened; he could hear only the distant noise of the river. That food . . . he could no longer see it, but he knew where it was. The window was just about wide enough to crawl through. He did so, feeling for the stone table and finding it. And the loaf . . . He tore it in half and broke bits off to chew. The bread was coarse and dry, but satisfying for all that. He found the meat, too; it tasted like cold pork. His hand touched something else, an earthenware jug, and when he lifted it, it gurgled. He tried it cautiously. Wine! A bit on the sour side, but it quenched his thirst. After eating an apple, he was quite full. And very tired. There was obviously no point in trying to go on further in the dark; he might as well bed down here. There were stone flags under his feet, but when he probed a little further, the surface was more yielding. Beaten earth, he guessed. Not exactly a feather bed, but weariness made a good mattress. He curled himself up on the ground. He wondered again where he was—or when—and what had happened to Brad; but not for long before he fell asleep.

His sleep was heavy. When he awoke, it was to a lancing brightness; he opened his eyes and immediately closed them against the dazzle of early sunlight. Shielding with his hand, he was aware of the sun's rays streaming in through the small window.

He took in his surroundings. It was a single room, about twelve feet square and no more than seven or eight feet high. Around the walls oblong stone boxes were stacked on shelves in tiers. The only furnishings were the stone table on which were the remains of the food he had eaten and another longer stone table carrying one of the boxes. There was a sickly, sweetish smell; he had been aware of it last night, but it seemed much stronger now.

Simon got to his feet and went to the table with the

box. It was between five and six feet long, two or three feet across, a couple of feet in depth. The top was open, but a lid of stone, rimmed with what looked like lead, lay beside it.

Inside the box was a statue, or rather a kind of high relief; the surround was white stone, but a human figure rose out of the centre. It was the effigy of a sleeping woman, hands folded on her breast, dressed in a white robe. Behind her head were ranged small jars and glass bottles with silver tops, a comb and silver-backed brush. Weird, he thought. He put a finger to the white surround. It wasn't stone but something softer. Plaster of paris?

The figure had been brilliantly carved. In the dimness, the folds of the robe looked like real cloth. And the curve of the pale cheek . . . a youngish woman, in her twenties probably, and pretty. He touched the cheek with his finger, too, and at once whipped it away, in horror. That wasn't stone either. It had indented under the light pressure of his finger: not stone, but cold dead flesh.

He knew now what place he was in: a charnel house, with coffins ranged all around and this latest one not yet sealed. The food and wine had been left as grave gifts, along with the ornaments and toilet articles. He had an urge to be sick, an absolute need to get out. The aperture by which he had entered was the only exit. Simon scrambled through it, kicking the stone table away behind him, not caring what noise he made. He fell out into the open, picked himself up, and stood for a moment deeply breathing in fresh air. The next thing he knew, there was a heavy step beside him, and before he could turn around to see who it was, an arm was against his throat like an iron bar, bruising and choking.

The events that followed were confusing and unpleasant. There were three other men apart from the one who had half choked him, and they drove him up a hill, belabouring his legs with sticks. There was a house at the top, but he was too dazed to have any impression beyond the fact that it was large and rectangular in shape. A wooden trapdoor was opened at the base of a wall, and he found himself being thrown down into a cellar. He hit the ground with a thump that slammed the breath from his body. The trapdoor slammed shut, leaving him in near blackness.

Someone already down there spoke to him in gibberish. He saw no point in trying to answer, and the other did not persist. He started trying to work things out. He had been discovered emerging from a family tomb. And tombs, everywhere and at all times, carried a heavy taboo, which he had, unwittingly, broken. He had, in fact, committed sacrilege, and whatever sort of society this was, punishment was liable to be severe.

His companion started talking again. It was still gibberish, but by repetition some bits took on significance. One phrase, for instance, spoken with the inflection of inquiry. "Foggy tea wash?" Something like that. Simon thought about the possible punishment. In a primitive society it could well be death, which put a very high premium on any possibility of escape.

He felt his way round the cellar, inch by inch. The walls were of brick, the bricks smaller than the ones he was accustomed to, but very firmly cemented in. He broke a fingernail on one. Brick, and then wood. A door: That was something. He went over it, inch by inch. It was of heavy timber, barred with iron. He found an iron lock, a keyhole, a heavy metal ring. After a long time of trying, he had to accept the fact that it was either locked or bolted on the other side, and that no one short of a superman was going to get it open from here.

The only other interruption in the brick was the hatch to the outside, through which they had been thrown. That was of heavy timber, too, and as firmly bolted. The glimmer of light round the edges was wafer-thin. The increasing stuffiness showed how little even of air it admitted.

During his exploration, the man with him had stayed where he was but with occasional bursts of unintelligible speech. "Foggy tea wash" occurred several times, still with the note of inquiry. He was asking if Simon was a foggy tea wash. Foggy, or fuggy? It came to him suddenly, a recollection of a hot afternoon and old Gargoyle (George Argyle, junior Latin master) droning on. *Fugitivus*—a runaway. More specifically, a runaway slave!

Things fell together. He was in the past, all right, and within a few hundred years he could place just when. Roman Britain.

In a fit of enthusiasm he answered, or tried to. *"Non fugitivus sum."* That produced blankness, followed by a meaningless flood. He tried *"Homo liber,"* to which the silence was longer still. Respectful, or simply uncomprehending? A renewed surge of what must be Latin was no help. Simon gave up, wishing he had paid more attention to the Gargoyle's soporific nasal tones. The one thing clear was that the man with him was almost certainly a Roman slave and naturally assumed that he was a slave, too, and a runaway. A runaway who had broken into a tomb and eaten the food meant to sustain the deceased lady while she got ready for her crossing of the Styx. His companion had another go, but Simon felt altogether too depressed to attempt an answer.

Much later the hatch was briefly opened and bread was thrown in—a couple of small loaves—and a leather flask containing water. He was able to see that the day was almost gone and, in the shadowy evening light, that his companion was a small, thin, undernourished man with a straggly grey beard. Simon picked up his loaf from the floor and wolfed it, and the pair of them shared the water in the flask. More time dragged by; he slept and woke and slept again. Then the hatch was pulled open again, and this time it was morning.

They were shouted at from above. The old man heaved himself out, and Simon took the tip and followed suit. The same brawny individual was in charge of the party and supervised their tying up. A rope went round the neck and secured both wrists and ankles; you could hobble, but no more. He felt some relief about that. Surely no one would bother to tie someone up in order to chop his head off?

The house, he could now see, was a typical Roman villa out of history books. An open cart stood close by, with a couple of oxen between the shafts. They were made to scramble in at the back, and a guard jumped in with them. Then the high back was slammed up, there were cries and the crack of a whip, and the cart rolled off.

It was an interminable journey, in discomfort which gradually turned to agony. There was a slight relief when they turned onto a paved road, but it was rapidly lost in the new pain of cramp. Simon tried to struggle up to a squatting position, but a shout from the guard, leaning against the side of the cart, put a stop to that. He could see nothing outside the cart. The sun beat down harshly, and he was soon sweating, and soon after that the flies found him. They had been given neither food nor water, and thirst became a torment. You might, he reflected wretchedly, tie someone up in order to take him to another place to chop his head off—in which case you might not think it worthwhile feeding and watering him.

Eventually there were noises other than the creak and rattle of the wheels, the driver's occasional cry, the snorts of the oxen. The sound of other vehicles, other voices: the cries, unintelligible but unmistakeable, of street vendors. They were in town. Londinium? It seemed likely. Not a small town, certainly. It was quite a long time before the cart creaked to a halt, the high back was dropped, and they were half urged, half booted out.

They were in a large open square, surrounded by buildings. At the far end, beyond a crowded clutter of market stalls, the buildings were impressive in size, fronted by pillars and colonnades. The nearer ones were more ordinary, with small shopfronts at ground level. Near where the cart had stopped there was a wooden platform, a few feet high and about fifteen feet long. A well-dressed clean-shaven man stood on it, along with three bearded men, who were roped and naked. There was a crowd facing the platform, bidding for the men on display.

Simon and the other were urged, with cuffs, round to the rear of the platform. More slaves stood there waiting their turn for auction; not only men but women, and some children. They were in two batches, one of more than fifty people, the other comprising about half a dozen. It was to the latter they were directed. The man who had brought them ripped their clothes off, in one quick movement as far as the other man was concerned, but with more difficulty in Simon's case. He looked at the shirt and pants curiously for a moment, asked some meaningless question, then shrugged and left them.

The sense of shame was acute, but less than he would have expected. Public nakedness did not seem to matter so much, compared with the brutal reality that he was about to be sold as a slave. But that was a good deal better than being put to death.

THE DAY STAYED HOT and cloudless. Thirst, which he had been able to forget in the distraction of the journey's end, returned and tantalized more cruelly. This, it was borne in on him, was just one of the aspects of slavery. Simon thought of the world in which he had lived till . . . when? The day before yesterday? All those rights so confidently claimed: to work, to food and shelter, to life and liberty and the pursuit of happiness. A slave had nothing, except on his master's sufferance or whim. Assuming he had some value, he would be given water before he died of thirst, but the actual torment of thirst was unimportant. You topped up the oil in a car engine because if you let it run dry, a valuable possession became a worthless wreck. His value as a possession would bring him water—eventually.

Those in the main batch were taken, singly or in groups, to the other side of the platform and removed from there by their new owners. None was taken from the smaller group, seven in number, which included him. The first batch dwindled until the last two slaves, a woman with a child two or three years old, went. A few minutes later the auction was over.

The seven remained, crouched in the hot dust. Two soldiers guarded them. They produced bread and meat from pouches in their metal-skirted tunics, ate it with daggers, and drank wine from leather flasks, with no more regard for their charges than would have been paid to penned sheep in a country market.

Time passed, immeasurable. The guards straightened up suddenly as a small group approached them across the open space of the forum. They stood to attention and slapped hands on arms in salute. The leader was in his thirties, of medium height, well muscled, with a thin face and keen eyes. He wore a tunic with a light red cloak over it, fastened at the front by a gold pin. Two other men followed him respectfully.

His inspection of the seven naked figures was rapid. Four he immediately touched on the shoulder with a small black stick he carried; they included the man who had been brought in with Simon. He studied the remaining three more closely. Standing in front of Simon, he put the point of the stick under his chin, lifting his head. He stooped down and kneaded the muscles of Simon's right arm with hard, probing fingers; the act was impersonal but degrading. He stood back again, making a more general survey. Then he touched just one of the three with his stick, rapped out a few words of command, and with his two followers strode away across the forum.

A choice had been made, Simon realized, but what choice? It did not, anyway, have any immediate effect; the seven were mobilized as a group and marched away by the two guards, except that marching was scarcely the term to describe the ragged shuffling progress their roped ankles permitted. They left the forum at the nearest corner and went along a narrow street, crowded with people and horse-drawn vehicles. It was lined with shops—small boxlike rooms open at the front—selling a variety of goods: metalwork, pottery, cloths, cooked meats, wines. Smells were strong all the way, but particularly as they passed one with a display of leather goods. No one paid any attention to them, any more than they appeared to pay attention to the beggars, with a wide variety of deformities and mutilations, who squatted on the roadside, chanting for alms.

They turned a corner into another, slightly wider street. The whole of the left side was taken up by one massive building, with no windows at ground level and only narrow slits higher up. A prison? The blank front was broken at last by a stone archway, wide enough to take a cart, with wooden doors folded back from stone pillars and an armed guard on either side. They went through without challenge; through the dark tunnel beyond and into a vast sunlit square.

It was full of soldiers, practising weaponry and exercising. They were in a number of squads, under instructors. Simon saw a squad fighting in pairs with wooden swords, and another group heaving lances at dummy targets, roughly man-sized figures made of sackcloth. Not a prison but a barracks. Did that mean they had been press-ganged for military service? If it were so, things looked better again. Only marginally, but margins were becoming important.

There was a brief outburst from one of their guards,

and the two groups split. Simon, totally ignorant of what was said, followed the man on his left. A barked order, accompanied by a casual but stinging cuff to the side of the face, told him he had done the wrong thing. The guards seemed to find it amusing; they laughed, obviously at him, before they parted, directing their separate squads. The five who had been tapped by the officer's black stick went through a doorway on the left. Simon and the remaining slave were marched on.

His new companion was a small, swarthy man of about twenty. He had laughed with the guards, and he now rattled words off, grinning at Simon as he did so. A query of some sort. When Simon just looked at him, he shrugged and said something to the guard. The guard responded, in an almost amiable tone. It looked as though the pair of them had passed some selection procedure and qualified for a slightly improved status.

Their destination was a door in the end block, immediately facing the tunnel through which they had entered the barracks. Inside there was a hall, lit by oil lamps, with an iron-railed stone staircase leading up and doors on either side. They were led through one of them into a room lined with shelves. The guard barked a command, and since his companion came to a halt, Simon did the same. He had a moment's panic as the guard approached him with his dagger pointing. But in a quick movement the rope was severed at wrists and ankles. It slipped to Simon's feet as the other man was similarly released, and he stretched his head and shoulders, easing his cramped muscles.

The room was a clothing store. A storeman found things for them: underpants and a loose tunic of unbleached wool. Simon still had his own socks and sandals on, and the man stared at these with some interest, asking a question. When Simon indicated his inability to answer, he mimed taking them off and handed him a pair in exchange. They were fairly primitive: simply shaped leather soles, with a thong running between the first and second toes to loop around the ankle. The storeman studied his twentieth-century sandals for a moment or two, before tossing them into a barrel.

None of them seemed too surprised by his inability to speak Latin. But of course, the Romans never conquered the whole of Britain. They probably thought he was a Pict or a Scot, or one of the wild Celts from across the Irish Sea. The speculation was abandoned when they were taken from the clothing store to another room on the far side of the hall. It held trestle tables with wooden benches, capable of seating two or three hundred, and at the far end a kitchen from which emanated the unbearably wonderful smell of meat cooking. Cooks and cooks' assistants were busy there. Simon felt faint as they approached the area.

They were given water first, in rough earthenware pots. Meanwhile, food—beans with a little meat but a lot of gravy—was being put on platters; they were given one each, with a small loaf of bread. Simon could not remember any time in his life when food had smelled, or tasted, as good. He wolfed it greedily.

When they had finished, the guard set them on their way again: out of the dining room and up the staircase. On the third landing he indicated a doorway.

It was a very long room, at least fifty feet in length and fifteen feet across. It had narrow windows at intervals, unglassed but set with iron bars. The floor was concrete, the walls of whitewashed stone. Along the walls, at intervals of about four feet, concrete rectangles projected into the centre. They were raised a few inches from the floor, their dimensions about six feet by three, and any doubt as to their purpose was removed by the fact that at the head of each was a rolled mattress. Halfway along the room there was a gap in the concrete beds, making room for a stove with a chimney vented high in the wall.

The guard said a few more words and went out. They heard the slap of his feet, descending, on the stone stairs. The other man unrolled one of the mattresses and lay down on a bed. Simon, after a brief hesitation, followed suit, taking the bed opposite. The mattress was of something like sailcloth, with straw inside: not exactly luxury, but an improvement on bare concrete.

Through the barred window he could see blue sky and a fretted edge of white cloud. He took stock of his situation, looking on the bright side first. To start with, he was alive, something he would not have betted heavily on at most moments during the past thirty-six hours. He had been fed and watered, and he was no longer roped. He even had a bed to lie on.

Against that had to be set the fact that he was not a free man. He had apparently been pressed into service in the Roman army, and he doubted if they would be willing to offer him a discharge even if he knew how to set about asking for one. The guard had left the pair of them here, unguarded, but that didn't mean a lot. As far as he knew, the only way in or out was the main gate, and while the two armed soldiers there had not queried their being brought in, he had a feeling they might take a different view of his trying to walk out.

35

Someone really enterprising might, he supposed, look for other possibilities of escape. He didn't feel that enterprising at present; the fact that they had been left alone seemed to indicate that the guard had no great fear of either of them getting away. And that last unintelligible speech might have included a warning of what was likely to happen to them if they tried; his companion certainly seemed to be resigned to his situation.

No, it was better to wait and see what the future offered. It might be impossible to escape from the barracks, but they could not be kept in a barracks indefinitely. There must, at some stage, be contact with the outside world, and a reasonable chance of making a break for it. And by then he would have been able to get a hang of things; the world about him was at the moment almost totally strange but was bound to get more familiar and so easier to cope with.

It would be a help to pick up the language a bit; his three years of doing Latin should help there. He wondered, for the first time in hours, what had happened to Brad. Schools in America didn't do Latin, did they? Poor old Brad—he probably still had no idea where they were, or when. If he had survived, that was. The more Simon thought, the more he felt he had been lucky. Being plunged without warning into a barbarous past carried hazards he would never have guessed.

He wondered about what was happening at home, too. Presumably there would have been a search party when they failed to get back; would they still be combing the wood, or had they abandoned it by now? He remembered reading somewhere that thousands of people disappeared every year without trace. How many of them might have done so through an experience like theirs? There would never have been any record, of course. Anyone who did find himself in the past would have to try to survive without talking about his origin. In any period a story like that would only land one in a bin.

No, the thing to do was lie doggo and play it by ear. He stretched out on the bed. The others from this dormitory were probably out exercising in the square. He remembered his first day at boarding school. He had arrived before anyone else, and there, too, he had been shown into an empty dormitory and left to wait. Not quite as spartan as this place—truckle beds were some improvement on concrete blocks, and there had been no bars on the windows—but fairly bleak compared with his bedroom at home. And full of the lurking hazards and threats of a totally new way of life. There were quite a few differences between being a new boy in an English boarding school and being an unwilling recruit in the Roman imperial army, but enough resemblances to provide him with just the barest trace of badly needed confidence. It was cooler here than outside, but still very warm. He relaxed and stared up at the high whitewashed ceiling.

Simon was awakened abruptly from his doze by the clatter of feet and a surge of voices. He struggled to sit up and saw them pouring through the door in a flood. They sat down heavily on beds, pulled off boots and equipment, and stretched out, chattering. For the most part they were no more than medium height, but they all were strongly muscled and fit-looking. The majority, too, were dark and more or less swarthy; the tall red-haired man who was coming in now was an outstanding exception.

When he stopped at the end of the bed on which Simon was sitting, Simon thought it was because he had seen him staring and resented it. It was a bit late to look away, so he offered a smile instead. The redhead was not mollified. He mouthed a rush of Latin which was definitely not friendly. Simon put his hands up, gesturing noncomprehension. All that provoked was another burst, equally venomous. Simon shook his head, still smiling to show his good intentions. The blotchy face beneath the red thatch scowled more ferociously; the next moment the stranger had taken a step forward and swung a sidewinder which caught Simon below the left jaw and sent him sprawling into the space between the beds.

The blow did not knock him out but dazed him considerably. As he lay there, he registered that the redhead had put one foot on the side of the bed, a fairly obvious indication of possession. He realized the probable reason for both the diatribe and the assault. Unwittingly he had taken the Celt's bed (he must be a Celt with that colouring), and his smile, following his failure to respond to the bawling out, had been taken for defiance rather than propitiation.

However unjustified the blow, there was no point in making an enemy, especially at this early stage. Simon scrambled to his feet, smiled again, and this time held his right hand out. The Celt ignored the hand. His face looked meaner than ever, if that was possible. He rapped out more Latin. It sounded like an order. Simon would have been very inclined to obey, whatever it demanded, had he only been able to work out what was required. As it was, all he could do was go on smiling and hold both hands out, palms up, as a sign of helplessness.

He was never to know quite what he had done wrong. Perhaps the gesture he made resembled something derisory or obscene in the Celt's tribal background. What he *was* to learn was that Rufus (as the Celt was called) was permanently spoiling for a fight, the more so when the prospective opponent was smaller or weaker than himself. He leapt at Simon, bore him down against the next bed, and got his neck in a strangling armhold.

Propitiation having proved disastrous, there was nothing for it but to fight back. That was easier proposed than carried out, though. The Celt was several years older, taller and heavier and a lot more powerful. Simon plucked at the arm gripping his throat, but futilely. He tried to use his legs to get a purchase which would enable him to throw the Celt off, but they only thrashed helplessly. The band compressing his windpipe was like iron; he could not draw breath.

The Celt's face stared down into his, teeth showing in a wicked grin. The grip did not loosen. He could not possibly, Simon thought, intend to kill him merely for usurping a bed and then failing to answer something. He felt his ears roaring and saw the grin, as unremitting as the grip. But it could happen, he realized incredulously; it *was* happening.

He made another convulsive effort to kick out with his feet. It failed, and he felt weakness spreading through his body; it was so much easier to let go than to struggle. He was aware of relaxing, giving up, and aware that the strangling arm still tightened. Then, in near blackness, he felt the impact of another heavy blow. Someone else was attacking him, and he wanted to tell him not to bother; it was all over anyway.

Simon came chokingly back to life. The Celt had loosed his hold; in fact, he now lay sprawled on the other side of the bed, with a figure bent over him, arm raised ready to strike if the Celt tried to get to his feet. The redhead did not look as though he felt keen on trying.

Getting slowly to his own feet, Simon took stock of his rescuer. He was old, forty at least, his black beard speckled with white. He was no taller than Simon, possibly an inch shorter, but his chest and arms were enormous. He had a broad, ugly face, broken-nosed and deeply scarred on both the forehead and the right cheek. Under any other circumstances Simon would have reckoned him much more worth avoiding than the Celt. He was not even sure now, with that forbidding face apparently glaring at him, that the Celt had not just been smacked away because he had infringed this one's rights to do the killing around here.

The attempt to smile his way out of trouble had been a disastrous failure last time. Simon stood in front of the barrel-chested man trying not to show anything and trying to keep his knees from trembling. The stare was long and suspicious and only ended in an utterance that was part inquiry and part growl. Simon looked at him helplessly; at least he was not going to make the mistake of trying any more hand gestures.

To his astonishment the glare cracked into a broad grin, displaying broken and missing teeth. A hand tightened on his shoulder, but the grip was plainly friendly. The big man spoke again: *"Est mihi nomen Bos."*

That was amazing, too. For the first time since they had been catapulted into the past he understood something clearly. "My name is Bos." Smiling in return, Simon tapped his chest.

"Est mihi nomen Simonus."

Bos nodded approvingly, repeated "Simonus," and went on into a stream of growling Latin in which Simon was immediately lost. He had something tattooed on his chest: a fish? It didn't matter. Nothing mattered except that he had found, for the moment at least, an ally in this bewildering and frightening world.

IV

OVER THE NEXT FEW DAYS Simon hardly stopped congratulating himself on his luck in meeting Bos and on the fact that for some reason Bos liked him. Under his protection Simon felt very safe; it was obvious that no one in the dormitory was going to tangle with Bos if he could possibly help it. The Celt in particular kept well out of his way, contenting himself with a silent vicious glare at Simon when Bos happened not to be looking.

Nor was it just protection; he got help and guidance from the big man, too. By sticking close to him, Simon was able to pick up quickly the tricks and routines of barracks life. Even on the exercise ground Bos kept an eye on him, and the instructor, who spent a lot of time bawling out the other new recruit, gave Simon an easy time. He, too, though superior in rank, obviously did not want to run the risk of Bos's getting riled.

The advantages were manifold. Bos took him to get fitted with boots and tossed aside the first pair offered as unsatisfactory; the man issuing them was quick to produce another pair, over which Bos, after a close examination and some twisting of the leather with his powerful fingers, nodded satisfaction. And Simon noticed that when they queued for food, it was not only Bos who was given larger and better portions, but he as well.

Gradually he was picking up the language. Bos seemed to find his ignorance amusing. He willingly supplied the Latin name for things Simon pointed out and was patient in repetition. It was possible he felt flattered at being asked to help: Latin, as Simon was to learn, was not his native tongue, and while he was not at all stupid, his mental powers fell a long way short of matching his physical strength.

Towards the end of the second day on the exercise ground, while they were taking a short break, a supply cart rolled in through the main gate. Simon pointed to it, in inquiry. It was pulled by two white oxen, and he asked the name of the animals.

Bos grinned at him in an odd way.

"*Boves*," he growled.

Of course, Simon thought—how could he have forgotten that? He remembered old Gargoyle explaining the origin of the word *bovine*. From *bos, bovis*—an ox. Bos was still grinning with delight, and suddenly he got it. Bos! He pointed to the animal and then to the man.

"*Tu—bos!*"

Bos roared with laughter, slapping his hands on his huge chest. He was obviously proud of the name he had acquired.

The training was partly general physical exercising, partly weapon training. Simon was given a wooden sword and in the first instance had to wield it against a wooden dummy, called a *palus*. He slashed away enthusiastically but a bit aimlessly, and the instructor had to put him right as to the kind of thrust or slash that was needed and the appropriate spots to aim at.

Simon for his part did his best to follow instructions. He realized that there was an ultimate objective—that the skills he was learning were meant to be applied in due course to blows not against a lump of man-shaped wood, but against a live human being. He did not let his mind dwell on that prospect. Before an army went into battle, it had to get to the place where the fighting was to take place, and once they were clear of the barracks, he would have a chance to slip away. The position after that was uncertain, but better than what might happen if he remained a soldier; and he was learning more and more as time went by.

Enough Latin, for instance, to be able to conduct a limited conversation with Bos. Bos, it appeared, came originally from the north and had been captured as a boy by a Roman raiding party. He told Simon his real name but, when Simon made a hash of repeating it, merely shrugged. Bos was good enough. Simon tried to find out what had happened to him between then and now, but communication failed. He persisted: How was it that he had become a soldier—*miles Romanus*?

Bos was bewildered. His big face creased in total non-comprehension. Simon racked his mind and his limited Latin to get it over to him. Start at the simplest level. Soldiers—he gestured, indicating both the two of them and the rest—they were all soldiers, Roman soldiers.

"*Milites?*" With understanding came amusement, starting as a slow grin but turning into belly-shaking laughter. When the paroxysm was over, Bos said something Simon did not follow, and then spoke more slowly and deliberately: "*Milites non sumus, Simonus. Gladiatores sumus!*"

It was Simon's turn to be staggered, but when he did grasp it, there was no impulse to laugh. Barracks and military training meant army; he had taken that for granted. He had completely forgotten about the Roman gladiators, who also had lived in barracks and trained with weapons. So much for his notion of deserting once the legion abandoned barracks life for active service. This was a legion that went from its barracks to the circus—the circus where there were no clowns, but bloody hand-to-hand combat, with loser left dying in the dust and winner gaining no more than a reprieve. He had got it wrong about the events that day in the forum. His little group had not been left behind to be press-ganged by the army; they had been sold as a block to the director of the local gladiatorial school.

Bos recognized his unhappiness and, though surprised by it, did his best to offer sympathy. Simon had the usual difficulty in making out what he was trying to convey, but repetition of the word *felix* made him realize Bos was telling him he was lucky. He showed his scepticism, and Bos ploughed on, in ponderous and barely intelligible explanation.

He was talking about Simon and the other who had arrived in the dormitory with him; they were lucky to have been picked for the school, to have been strong enough to train as gladiators. Especially Simon, who, although he was tall and not a weakling, was young to have gained acceptance. Because of that, he had a chance. He would have a sword, an opportunity to defend himself. Not like the others who had been marched to the barracks that day. He spat in the dust, a gesture indicating their fate.

Simon thought of the five who had crouched naked beside them throughout that broiling afternoon, especially of the little old man who had been in the cellar with him. What was going to happen to them? he asked Bos.

Bos shrugged. *"Damnati ad bestias."*

Simon had enough Latin to know what that meant. Condemned to the beasts—sent out into the arena, weaponless, to be savaged and eaten by starving lions, for the amusement of spectators. He almost did feel he was lucky.

During the ensuing days and weeks, Simon gradually got the hang of his new way of life. At the top, with absolute authority, was Gaius Turbatus, the *lanista*, or director of training. This was the man in the red cloak who had picked Simon out in the forum. He appeared frequently but at unpredictable intervals, sometimes accompanied by his deputies, sometimes alone. He studied the recruits very carefully, observing their progress with a keen, cold eye. Certain men were dismissed from the ranks following a word from him to an instructor, and did not reappear. They had been condemned to the beasts, too, Bos explained, having failed to make the grade as gladiators.

The trainers were mostly superannuated gladiators. Apart from general training, they supervised the individual disciplines, of which there were many different kinds. Some, whose training took place not in the square but in an arena behind the barracks, had to do with horses; like the *essedarii* who fought from horse-driven chariots. All the rest fought on foot, but in a number of ways.

There were several varieties of heavily armed fighter, under the general title of *secutores*. A *secutor parmularius* had a small shield, for instance, while a *scutarius* had a big one. And there were *thraeces*, who had light shields and a sort of sickle, and the *retiarii*, who were by way of being the stars of the show. These wore neither helmet nor breastplate—they fought bareheaded in tunics—and were armed only with a net with which to snare their opponents, a three-pronged trident, and a small dagger. Apparently they took on not only heavily armed foot fighters but even *essedarii*. Their skill and therefore their advantage lay in their agility; their aim was to dance round their more powerful foe, provoking and angering and eventually exhausting him—only then did they move in, tangle him in the net, pin him with the trident, and dispatch him with the dagger.

Simon, Bos said, was not the right type for a *retiarius*— too heavily built, young as he was, and not fast enough on his feet. Simon did not feel any great regret over that judgement. He did not relish the notion of going into the arena at all, but if he had to, he wanted to have something more than a yard or two of netting to protect him.

There were a lot of other people in the barracks, apart from the gladiators and their trainers and the poor devils in the north wing who had nothing to do but wait for their appointment with the lions. (And tigers and wolves, Bos added, and occasionally the chance of being trampled to death by maddened elephants, though that was something of a rarity.) There was a host of auxiliaries, playing their separate parts in this little world: cooks and their assistants, storemen, bootmakers, tailors, armourers, masseurs, doctors, and medical orderlies . . . they seemed to outnumber the gladiators, but it wasn't easy to estimate their numbers accurately. For one thing they had the right to pass in and out of the barracks without restriction. Simon had a thought of getting out himself by passing as one of them, but abandoned it; however hard he found it to keep track, the guards seemed to know them all, and a botched escape, he was fairly sure, would, like a poor showing in training, condemn him to the beasts.

He did not try to discuss any of this with Bos. Even with their limited comprehension of each other's speech, he had come to realize that Bos's basic attitude was one of acceptance of things as they were. After being taken captive as a boy, he had been a farm slave for many years before being sold to the gladiatorial school on the death of his master. For several years since, he had fought as a *secutor*, surviving dozens of single-handed combats and several mass battles. None of this, obviously, would he have chosen, but he did not seem to resent any of it and would, Simon guessed, have thought anyone mad who suggested trying to escape from it.

But while he could not confide his own intentions to Bos, he could learn from him. He learned, for instance, that the present rigid confinement to barracks normally applied only to those like himself who had not yet fought: the *tirones*. The *veterani*, such as Bos, were usually permitted to go in and out, as the auxiliaries did. The exception to this was in the month immediately leading up to the Games.

So once the Games were over, there would be a relaxation, and by that time, too, he would be a *veteranus*. Bos talked, with anticipation but not impatiently, of the things and places he would show Simon in the city; it was Londinium as he had assumed. There was a little wine bar in particular which was Bos's home, insofar as he could ever know one. His girlfriend kept it. She would like Simon, he said. *And* she had a young sister. He made a gesture indicating feminine beauty and winked an eye.

Simon played up to this. The important thing was getting out of the barracks. It was safer to keep his counsel as far as the step after that was concerned. One thing of which he was sure was that, however attractive the wine bar or the younger sister, they could not begin to make up for the unpleasantness of staying on as a gladiator.

Or the risks. He reminded himself of something else: Everything depended on his actually making the transition from *tiro* to *veteranus*—in other words, on fighting at the games and winning. Whatever his intentions for the future, fitness and skill as a gladiator were important *now*. It was not something like a school examination or cricket trials which loomed ahead, but a matter of life and death. *His* life.

With that in mind, Simon put effort into the training in a way he never had for anything before, and would scarcely have thought himself capable of doing. He exercised and practised not only during the long periods scheduled by the *lanista,* but outside them as well. Bos heartily approved, joining him and encouraging him. As he frankly said, other things being equal, the odds were not on Simon's side. The greatest fatalities were always (and understandably) among the *tirones*; in addition, Simon was a lot younger than was usual and, although tall and reasonably well built, was a long way from peak condition. So Bos welcomed the enthusiasm and drove Simon on when he showed any sign of flagging.

Bos also used his influence with the cooks to get Simon even more of the precious meat which in one meal a day accompanied the basic mess of barley and beans. Simon became an object of professional pride to him; he would stare at him with the approval of a farmer surveying a prize steer.

The other and even more important thing he did was to teach the tricks of his trade—the manoeuvres and dodges he had learned in the long years of fighting. He had already fixed it that Simon, after the initial basic training, should join him as a *secutor parmularius*. The advantage of having a lighter and less cumbersome shield, he declared, more than made up for the lower level of protection even when one was up against a *scutarius,* and against a *retiarius* the difference was much more marked. Especially, he added, for a youngster like Simon.

There was one particular trick he would reveal only when they were off parade, with no one watching. It was for use against a *retiarius*, as a last resort if one had been netted, and involved falling in a particular way, rolling, and coming up again with a special leap which took you sufficiently clear of your opponent to have a chance to cut your way free of the net. Bos managed to get hold of a net for them to practise with in one of the unused storerooms. It was agonizingly difficult, involving the use of muscles Simon had not imagined existed. Practising went on a long time before Bos expressed grudging satisfaction.

Something else happened in the aftermath to this, while they were relaxing and resting. Bos's barrel chest rose and fell with his breathing, and the fish design on it did the same. At the beginning Simon had wondered idly about the tattoo, but later it had become something he took for granted, like the trumpet reveille soon after dawn or the grainy coarseness of the bread. In the beginning he would have felt diffident about asking, but he felt more sure now of Bos's amiability.

Bos did not look surprised or put out by the question. He said simply: *"Christianus sum."*

It should not have been too much of a surprise; Simon recalled that the fish had been one of the earliest Christian symbols. It was just that he did not easily associate the remark with someone like Bos—especially with someone of Bos's calling. How did he reconcile being a Christian with a lifetime commitment to kill people in the arena? He decided it would be unwise, especially with his limited command of Latin, to pursue that point. He contented himself with saying: *"Et ego."* Bos looked at him, and this time was surprised. Simon nodded. *"Christianus sum."*

The big face split into a grin, and a moment later he was enfolded in a hug that made him feel Bos ought to have been called after a bear rather than an ox. He did not grasp all, or even half, of what else was said except that Bos was going to take him to meet a priest, after the Games. That might be useful, Simon thought. Whatever the priest thought about Bos's being a gladiator, surely he would lend a hand to help someone else to escape from the business. He wondered again, just where in the past he was. Before Christianity took over, presumably, but he had forgotten when that happened. And it scarcely mattered, compared with what lay not much more than a week ahead.

Although Bos was his close and constant companion, Simon had inevitably come to know other people in the barracks, particularly in the dormitory. Apart from the Celt, who kept his distance, he got on well with all of them, though he realized that might well be connected with the fact that Bos had befriended him.

The one he got on best with was Tulpius, the slave who had been picked with him out of the seven in the forum. In such a world as this, shared experiences—common disasters and common strokes of luck—were very likely to forge bonds of real, if transient, friendship. At any rate, he talked quite a bit with Tulpius, who was unlike Bos in having been a *verna*, a slave from birth, bred on a big country estate. He, too, had been sold, not on the death of his master, but on the dissolution of the estate. He was vague about the reason for it—there had been some talk of a fortune's being lost in sea-trading ventures. The result was all that mattered. He had found himself in a much smaller household, and in the city, not the country. He had not liked it; there had been only six slaves altogether, which meant a lot more work than he had been used to.

Then his new master had been murdered. There was no evidence as to who had killed him—he had been stabbed in the street, just outside the house. It was lucky that it had happened outside rather than inside. The magistrates had varied the normal ruling that all slaves of a murdered man should be put to death (for not having protected him) and had ordered that only the chief slave should be executed out of hand. The rest had been sold to the *lanista*. He had been lucky again in being young and strong enough to be chosen for the sword, instead of going like the rest to the beasts.

Bos had not shown any interest in Simon's life prior to joining the gladiatorial school—he had very little curiosity in general—but Tulpius did ask questions. Simon's near-total ignorance of the language immediately stamped him as a barbarian—someone from foreign parts. So he said he hailed from a land across the sea, leaving it vague as to whether he meant Ireland or Scandinavia or Ultima Thule, and had been captured by pirates and sold here in Britain. Tulpius found that acceptable; just another run-of-the-mill story of life in the Roman Empire. He asked other questions about his earlier life, and Simon duly invented what he could and fell back on his poor Latin when things started looking sticky. But they rarely did; very little was known of lands beyond the borders of the empire, so almost anything would do.

The weather had been unsettled for a week, and a lot of the final practising had taken place in pouring rain, but the day of the Games dawned fine. Simon awoke to the trumpet call with a strange feeling of excitement mixed with fear and a dragging sense of doom. The meal the night before had been a special one, with an extra ration of meat, and even jugs of wine passed from hand to hand along the trestle tables. There had been a lot of jollity and laughter and much bellowing of songs. Simon had put up a show of joining in, but had been acutely aware of the macabre nature of a situation in which men now singing and laughing together would tomorrow be intent on killing one another.

The day of reckoning had come, and he felt a sick conviction that all the effort had been inadequate and to no purpose. There was a different atmosphere in the dormitory—a quietness and tenseness and preoccupation in place of the usual jesting and horseplay. And the others were all older than he was, most of them a lot older, and most of them experienced. Bos put a hand on his shoulder and gave him a grin and a word or two of encouragement, but even he was grim-looking and taciturn. It was a weird and awful thing to look out into the morning light, with the sun rising over the east wing of the barracks, and know that the odds were one wouldn't live to see it set.

They marched in procession from the barracks to the circus, with armed guards marching alongside. That put paid to any notion of escape on the way. Although it was early, the streets were lined with people, some cheering, others jeering. Simon wondered if Brad might be among them, but thought it highly unlikely. He doubted if Brad had even survived, but if he had, it could be only as a slave, not as one of the city mob enjoying the festival. Though that would be preferable to what he faced.

The circus presented itself as a high blank curving wall, with an open gate at the base through which they marched into a dark tunnel, lit by torches fixed against the sides. The tunnel sloped down and then, after a time, up again. They came out, blinking sunlight from their eyes, into the arena, and to a great roar from the spectators massed in tiers all round. As far as Simon could tell, not a seat was empty. The procession wheeled towards a place at the centre of one of the long sides of the amphitheatre, where a platform jutted out with a purple awning and purple-draped front. The figure sitting in the middle, in a purple toga, would be the governor. They marched beneath him, arms raised in salute, and bellowed the ritual greeting: *"Morituri te salutamus!"* We who are about to die salute thee.

Simon opened his mouth obediently, but nothing came out. Sand crunched underfoot, golden in the sunlight.

There would be a lot of red staining it, before the day was over.

Having completed a circuit, they were marched back into the shadows; as they entered the tunnel, Simon heard the growling and snarling of the wild beasts penned on one side, and caught their rank feral smell. Hours of waiting still lay ahead. The morning was devoted to the beasts, either fighting between themselves or slaughtering their helpless human victims. Light entertainment—clowns and jugglers and such—came next. Then, in the afternoon, the important show. Their show.

Simon had been separated from Bos during the procession, but the big man came and found him after they had been dispersed into one of the long, low cavernous rooms that lay on either side of the central tunnel. He said: "Good news!"

Simon looked at him. The only good news he could imagine, apart from a miraculous reappearance of the fireball with late-twentieth-century England on the far side, would be that the Goths and Vandals were pounding at the city gates. Bos said: "You're going to be fighting another *tiro*, not a *veteranus*."

He supposed that was better than nothing. "Who?"

Bos shrugged his broad shoulders. "Not a *veteranus*, that's what matters. I told Burro"—that was the instructor—"that you were too promising a youngster to be chopped without a chance of proving yourself. He put it up to the *lanista*, and the *lanista* has agreed." He slapped Simon's arm. "Now, let's see you be a credit to me!"

Even though Simon was scarcely looking forward to what came next, time passed with wearisome slowness.

Down here they could hear no sounds from the arena, but Simon could imagine the carnage. He felt sick at the thought, and when they were brought a snack—bread and cold stringy meat—he at first refused it. But Bos was not standing for that; a slice of meat, he growled, could make the vital difference to a swordsman's fitness—the difference between killer and killed. Simon choked, but managed to swallow it.

Then, unexpectedly, horrifyingly, the time had come. They were marched out, to another roar of welcome from the crowd. They paraded again, but this time with a musical accompaniment; an orchestra, of trumpets, horns, flutes, and stringed instruments, went ahead of them, playing something like a march. They made their gruesome salute to the governor a second time, had it acknowledged by the languid wave of a handkerchief, and the greater part of the column headed back towards the tunnel. Those were the fighters for the later bouts. When his section was halted, Simon realized with a churning stomach that he was one of those who were on first.

There were to be four simultaneous contests of *secutor* against *retiarius*, in four different corners of the arena. The star turn took place directly beneath the governor's dais and was supervised by the *lanista*. Simon was directed by one of the *lanista*'s deputies to the eastern end. He waited there, gripping his sword tightly, while the *retiarii* were directed to their stations, too.

He recognized his opponent the moment he started to walk forward but hoped he was mistaken—that such a bad joke could not be true. But it was Tulpius who stood and faced him, net in his left hand, trident poised in the right.

The orchestra had remained in the middle of the arena.

They were playing again: jangling angry music that clawed at one's nerves. He looked at Tulpius, at a set, tense face which showed no sign of recognition. The music went on and on, to surges of impatient howling from the crowd. It reached a crescendo and abruptly stopped. For a second or two there was silence, even the spectators seeming to hold their breath. Then a shrill blast of trumpets and a full-throated roar of satisfaction. The contests had begun.

Tulpius moved catlike, circling him. Simon turned with him, on the same spot. The circling went on and on. Suddenly Tulpius darted forward, net flung upwards, babbling a stream of venomous Latin. Simon dodged back, the falling net brushing against his shield arm. The circling started again.

Time ceased to mean anything; there was only a never-ending succession of moments in which concentration had to be held and honed. At some point a shout from the spectators, marking the early end of one of the other bouts, distracted him momentarily. The net flashed and almost had him, and as he stepped back, he nearly tripped and fell. The taunting continued all the time. He felt at a disadvantage in not being able to reply, but at least he could not understand much of what was being said, either, even though the tone was all too clear. He thought of Tulpius the previous evening, passing him the jug of wine and offering a toast to friendship. The net flashed, and he quickly pulled back.

It was the net which, gradually, became his obsession. It maddened and mesmerized him; he wondered if this was what happened to a bull in front of a matador's cloth. He saw, was conscious of, nothing but the net. That was the real tormentor rather than the man wielding it. Even more than the constant turning and dodging, the net seemed to be draining strength from him. The urge to slash it with his sword, to put an end to its weaving and flicking, increased with every moment. In the end it was uncontrollable. His right arm moved almost as though it were something separate, with a will and a need of its own. The sword flashed out towards the mocking net.

The net shifted, whirled through the air, twisted, and came down. Simon felt it over his head, light and insubstantial for an instant but turning into knotted cord that tightened and twisted and pulled him irresistibly. He was off-balance, and going down, and once down, it would be as good as over.

Surprisingly he felt clearheaded. Uppermost in his mind was the thought not of his impending death, but that Bos would be disappointed. Bos . . . He remembered the hours of practice in the storeroom. The rolling fall first, with sword held back . . . He hit the ground and rolled. Then the leap. He tensed his muscles, gathered breath, exploded upwards. He landed on his feet, swayed, tottered, but stayed upright. The net still covered him but only loosely; the leap had dragged it out of Tulpius's grasp. Simon slashed upwards with his sword, and it parted and fell.

He heard the crowd roaring all round. Tulpius stood a few paces away, his face frozen now with fear, holding the trident. He did not move as Simon attacked, and the sword's edge sent the trident clattering yards away.

The *lanista*'s deputy was beside him, shouting something. He did not know what it was, and did not care. The crowd was shouting, too—not only those immediately above but all round the arena, it seemed. It was a concerted chant, like that of football crowds—a single word over and over again. Not *missos*—set him free—but *iugula*. Cut his throat. . . .

The deputy seized Simon's arm and dragged him round. He was pointing to the dais where the governor sat. It was a long way off, but the gesture was unmistakeable. Thumb pointed to chest: Dispatch him. The bout underneath the dais had ended, too. The *retiarius* stood victorious. An attendant in a mask stood over the fallen *secutor*, reaching down with a hot iron, making sure the man was dead. The shouts went on and on. "*Iugula . . . iugula . . . iugula. . . .*" The deputy *lanista* was shouting, too. Simon dropped his sword and turned away.

Two days later he squatted naked in the dust of the forum. There had been a thunderstorm during the night, but the sun beating down from a sky of naked blue had already dried the ground, and the heat was rapidly becoming oppressive. He was roped as before, along with more than a score of others. From the auction platform behind them he heard the auctioneer's urgings and the bids for the slave on show.

Simon thought of his last meeting with Bos, the big hand grasping his through the bars of the cell. Bos had been troubled, bitterly disappointed, but, above all, uncomprehending. Simon had been his pupil, with a great future as a *secutor*, and Simon had let him down. He could not understand why.

And even if he had had enough Latin, Simon doubted if it would have been possible to explain. This was a totally different world, and killing, for a long time, had been Bos's profession. Bos went on to say something else and, by dogged repetition, finally got it across. He had been able to do Simon one last favour. He had pleaded with the *lanista*, having won his own contest well, and the *lanista* had listened to him. Instead of being condemned to the beasts, Simon would be sold off in the market.

To Bos himself, it was plain, there was not much difference between the two fates. A *secutor* who had failed to kill after winning a bout might as well be dead. Simon, on the other hand, was very much aware of the difference, and grateful to his unhappy friend. To be safe from the beasts and out of the gladiatorial school as well was more than he could have hoped for. Whatever fate lay in store for him as a slave was better than those.

The guard came and prodded him to his feet. He shuffled round to the other side of the wooden screen and mounted the steps to the platform. The auctioneer, a tall man with a thin, greasy-looking face, gave an order and, when Simon failed to respond, roughly pulled up first one arm, then the other, and turned him round. He was being shown off, he realized, from all angles. The auctioneer launched into what was presumably a catalogue of his qualities. Simon avoided looking at the people clustered in front. The sense of relief in being no longer a gladiator was not strong enough to survive this particular experience. All he could feel was shame.

They were bidding for him. Someone came up close and stared at him, and he looked blindly at the sky. A last bid, a final entreaty from the auctioneer, and it was over. The guard pushed him to the steps and down to where his new owner waited.

He was aware of two figures, a man and a boy, both in embroidered tunics of expensive cloth. He still would not look at them, but bowed low as he had seen other slaves do. It was the boy who responded. He said, in English:

"Pretty good, Simon. That saves you from a whipping. For today anyway."

V

THE VILLA WAS BUILT on a small plateau just under the brow of a hill and faced southeast. All that Simon had so far managed to take in was an impression of spaciousness and luxury. He sat with Brad in the *impluvium*, the central courtyard, or rather, they reclined on facing couches, made of intricately carved oak and heaped with cushions. When he moved, he was aware of the clinging softness of the tunic he had been given, to replace the blanket he had worn during the drive out from the city.

A servant brought a painted tray with a tall jug of rosy glass and two elegant glass beakers, and set it down on the small table between them. Brad reached and poured for them both. He raised his glass.

"*Prosit!* Which means, I believe: May it do you good." He sipped. "Not bad?"

It was basically lemon, but with other spicy flavours as well. Taste buds, battered almost to extinction by the barracks diet, came gratefully back to life. Simon said: "Better than not bad. Now tell me how it happened—all this."

During the journey here, on Brad's prompting, he had told his own story. He had not needed much encouragement; the relief of talking to someone who could understand what he said had made him garrulous. But curiosity was uppermost now.

Laconically, Brad set about telling him. The horsemen who had picked him up at the edge of the wood had been returning from a hunting party. They had given chase more out of curiosity than anything else. But having captured him, they thought they might make a coin or two out of selling him. They decided to stay overnight at an inn and take him into the city the following morning.

Simon said: "Wait a minute." Brad looked at him. "How did you know all this—what they were planning to do?"

"Because they were discussing it. I was facedown over a saddlebow, but I could hear well enough."

"Are you telling me they were talking *English*?"

Brad smiled. "I guess maybe they had a bit of an English accent, being natives of this island, but no, they spoke regular Latin."

"But . . . I thought they didn't do Latin in American schools?"

"They don't often. We didn't study it in my school. I got interested a couple of years back and studied it in my leisure time. I wouldn't say I got really proficient, but I could make out what these characters were saying."

Simon recalled thinking of poor Brad's having to cope

with an incomprehensible world, and felt a wave of irritation. He said briefly: "Go on."

The men had kept Brad with them at the inn and bought him supper when they had their own. They hadn't seemed a bad bunch, Brad thought, but a runaway slave was fair game, and a useful bonus after an unsuccessful hunting trip. After eating, they sat on in the dining room, drinking wine and playing dice. There was another guest in the room, a man on his own. He was at the next table, but not far from Brad, and Brad saw him looking with some curiosity, not so much at him as at his jeans. The others hadn't spotted them as unusual or, if they had, had not thought it worth comment.

The stranger asked them where they had found Brad, and they told him, and that they were taking him into the city to sell. The man looked as though he might be on the point of saying something, but in the end did not. He got to his feet, preparing to retire.

In a low voice, in Latin, Brad said: "I can tell you wonders." He hesitated, looking from Brad to the men and back, but in the end he smiled regretfully and shook his head. As he started to turn away, there was a little chink of metal, and Brad saw something hanging from a chain round his neck: a gilt cross.

In an even lower voice, but loud enough to carry, Brad said: *"Christus ascensus est."* Christ is risen.

That worked. The man with the cross turned back. He started negotiations with the horsemen which did not take long. Both sides knew roughly what price a boy of Brad's age and physical condition would fetch in the open market. Brad had become the property of Quintus Cornelius Ericius, the man who that morning had bought Simon, too.

There were a lot of questions that needed asking, but the one this raised could not wait. Simon asked: "How did that happen anyway? I mean, how did you know I'd be there. Or was it just accidental?"

"We got people asking around. I figured you'd probably wind up in the slave market, and we kept a check on it for a time. There aren't that many slaves around who don't speak the language, and the age thing narrowed it down further. We drew a blank, and I thought maybe you'd got killed. You don't need telling that human life carries a lower price tag than where we came from. Then about a week ago someone who knows Quintus Cornelius, and knew he'd been looking for a barbarian boy, got talking in the baths to Gaius Turbatus . . ."

"The *lanista!*"

"That's right, the guy who runs the gladiators' school. He was talking about a young barbarian he'd got who showed promise as a *secutor*—said he was worth betting on. It sounded interesting. And when you pulled that sensation in the arena . . ."

"Were you there?"

Brad shook his head. "The circus is off limits to Christians, and from what I've heard about the shows I've no regrets about that. But you were certainly the talk of the town, and even without telephones it's staggering how fast news travels around here. Quintus Cornelius didn't really think there was a chance; he said if they hadn't chopped you on the spot, they would have done so as soon as you got backstage. But he got someone to ask, and they said you were being sold off instead. So we took a trip to the forum, and the rest you know." He looked at Simon in amusement. "The beard almost threw me. Not exactly a thing of beauty, but confusing."

Simon fingered the growth on his chin. "I might keep it."

"You're in trouble. if you do. Beards are for slaves. Hadn't you noticed?"

"I thought it was gladiators."

"Gladiators and slaves. The not-free. Free men shave."

Simon wrinkled his brow. "I don't remember that in Roman history."

Brad's look was quizzical. "You don't?"

"We *are* free, I suppose? Quintus Cornelius . . ."

"Christians don't have slaves. Only servants. Mind you, I gather in some cases there's not a lot of difference. But Quintus Cornelius's servants seem to do OK. And we aren't servants anyway."

"What are we then?"

"Guests."

"For how long?"

Brad shrugged. In the rectangular pool that occupied the centre of the *impluvium*, water rose from two fountains and tinkled lazily back. Large golden fish swam among the water plants. Through the open roof one saw blue sky and a fragment of white cloud. The ceramic tiles had pictures of dolphins sporting in the waves, and there were paintings of saints on the walls. Simon had seen paintings very like them in the National Gallery. It was all calm and peaceful and luxurious, but something bothered him.

He said: "I don't know. . . ."

"What?"

"This household is a Christian one, right? And Quintus Cornelius is a rich man." Simon paused. "Back in gladiator school there was the man I told you about who helped me.

66

Bos. He was a Christian, too. But he was also a gladiator, and his profession was killing people."

"You could say the same about soldiers. A lot of those in our world were Christian."

"It's not the same. I've been trying to work out just where we are—or *when* we are. The fireball . . . we were pulled through it somehow into Roman Britain. Right?"

"Right."

"But what year? I can remember Constantine's date— he became sole emperor in 324. Christianity became the state religion after that, so we must have gone back before it. But it's a time in which Christians aren't being persecuted. And Bos seems to find no difficulty being both a Christian and a gladiator, which doesn't sound like early Christians to me."

Brad was grinning. "You'd like to know what year it is?"

"I don't suppose it makes much difference. But yes."

"No problem. Nineteen eighty-one."

"Come on! You mean, it's just a dream. Whose—yours or mine? I know I'm not dreaming."

"OK, let's figure it a little more closely. Christianity is not the state religion. So what is?"

"Well, they have lots of different gods. All those temples round the forum."

"Did you hear any of the gladiators swear 'by Julian'? Not Bos, of course, but the rest?"

"Yes."

"Who did you figure he was?"

"I didn't think. Julius Caesar? They made him a god."

"*Julianus*, not Julius. To be precise, Flavius Claudius Julianus. Born 331, emperor from 361 to 363. Julian the Apostate. He reversed Constantine's ruling about Chris-

67

tianity and restored paganism. But he'd been emperor
only two years when he went to war against the Persians.
He did well to begin with; then he was wounded in battle
and died of his wounds. The Christians took over again
and this time stayed in charge."

"I still don't see. . . ."

"I've been quoting from our history books, on the other
side of the fireball. On this side, things went differently.
Julian wasn't killed in his early thirties. He won that battle and went on to conquer the Persians. He did a few
other things, like bringing the government of the empire
back to Rome from Byzantium, where Constantine had
moved it. In fact, he totally reorganized the empire. He
didn't die until he was nearly eighty, and he'd gotten
things pretty stable by then. They've stayed that way."

Simon wondered if it could be some farfetched joke of
Brad's. But was being in a world that had never happened
very different from being trapped in the past? He said:
"An If world?"

"Except that from here the If world is the one we came
from. You try talking to people about things like the In-
dustrial Revolution and tanks and television and silicon
chips—not to mention simple things like there being a
pope in Rome instead of an emperor. Not easy, I can tell
you."

"You mean, you've tried? With Quintus Cornelius?"
Brad nodded. "Do you think that was wise?"

"I'm not quite sure yet. It happened. He was interested
in my jeans. He hadn't seen cloth like that before. And
then there was the zipper; that really got to him. He's
bright for an old guy, and open-minded for a Roman. He
questioned me: What land did I come from where they

did such ingenious metalworking? I could have tried lying, I suppose, and said it was from the same land where Pliny said men carried their heads underneath their arms, but I didn't think he'd buy that. And he'd done a lot for me already, so I wanted to be honest with him. Anyway, I decided to go for broke and showed him my watch— I'd managed to hide it in my jeans pocket before the others could spot it."

The watch, which had been a considerable source of envy to Simon, was a calendar quartz alarm chronometer. He tried to imagine the impact it would have on someone accustomed to telling time by sundials and water clocks. He asked: "What did he make of it?"

"He thought it was magic. It took him a long time to understand what it was meant to do—Arabic numerals never got invented in this world, so the readout didn't mean anything in itself, but the flashing digits fascinated him, especially when I demonstrated all the functions. The alarm in particular. One thing he knew for sure was that it hadn't come from any place in either the Roman or the Chinese empires, and it seemed even less likely that it had been made by barbarians. At that time I thought, like you, that we'd gone back into the past. Quintus Cornelius was ready to accept that I'd come from some distant future, as the least unreasonable of all the possible absurdities.

"Then, as we went on talking, the discrepancies started to crop up. Like dating. They date the way the Romans did before Christianity—A.U.C, not A.D. *Ab urbe condita*—from the founding of the city. And I discovered this Rome had been founded two and a half thousand years ago. And that Britain had been a Roman province for nearly two thousand years, not a couple of hundred. He got to it almost as soon as I did. Once you've accepted that someone has come from the future, I guess it's not too difficult switching that to a parallel world. As I say, he's open-minded for a Roman. It's probably to do with being a Christian. They're tolerated, but not really part of things."

Simon had been trying to come to grips with the situation. He said, feeling his way: "The Roman Empire never fell in this world. So . . ."

His words trailed off. Brad said: "So a whole lot of things. No Mohammed, for instance; or if there was one, he lived and died obscure. No Islam anyway. And it was probably out of Islam that the ideas came that led to the Renaissance and later to science and engineering. This world has scarcely changed in two thousand years. Some minor improvements—in glassmaking, for instance—but nothing fundamental."

"I still don't see how that could happen."

"Ancient Egypt lasted for thousands of years with almost nothing changing. So did China. We take rapid change for granted, but really it's pretty unusual. Static civilizations are probably more natural. And Julian—the Julian who survived—did a sound job in stabilizing his world. He completely reorganized both the army and the empire. Except for Jews and Christians, every citizen has to do military service. That turned the army back into a citizen army and got rid of the mercenaries. And he laid down a rule that no emperor could be succeeded by an emperor from the same province, though they always rule from Rome. On top of that he defused the Christian problem. That was probably the most important thing he did do."

"How do you mean—defused?"

"The basic problem was that the Christians and Jews believed in a single god and regarded it as the worst possible sin to worship or even acknowledge any other. But the Roman emperor was supposed to be a god, and everyone had to swear an oath to him. The Christians and Jews refused. It didn't matter so much about the Jews because after the Romans destroyed Jerusalem, they were scattered and survived only in isolated groups. But early Christianity was more widespread and dynamic. It got right to the heart of the empire; the chief bishop was the bishop of Rome. Christians were very noisy about refusing to bend a knee to the god-emperor. The ones who refused got martyred, and the martyrdoms converted more people to Christianity. As far as the Romans were concerned, it was a vicious circle.

"In this world, Julian fixed things neatly. He decreed that no living man could be deified, including the emperor. Including himself, in fact. So the oath of allegiance became just that, an acknowledgement to a ruler, not to a god. The Christians were tolerated instead of being persecuted—they're barred from public office, but that's not something to die for—and the movement ran out of steam. Julian was deified after his death—the last emperor who was, incidentally—but that didn't matter. It didn't bother the Christians, as long as they were left in peace to worship their own god."

Brad poured more of the lemon drink. There were plants in pots round the pool, some quite tall. A bird flew down through the open roof and settled on one. A sparrow; birds hadn't changed.

Simon said: "Thanks." The drink was very pleasant. The whole setup scored high for comfort, for luxury, in fact.

"What was the fireball, do you think? Nothing to do with ball lightning anyway."

Brad shook his head. "No. You'd need to be an Einstein even to understand how to set about trying to work it out. These parallel worlds exist side by side, occupying the same space and time, yet separate. That seems to require some basic underlying medium, like the old concept of aether. Maybe it can fray or warp in places, allowing two worlds to come into contact, and the fireball was that sort of fraying."

You'd need to be brighter, Simon thought, than he was to understand what Brad was talking about. He said: "So, do we wait for another one to come along and take us home?"

"Might be a long wait. And could we be sure we'd make it back to where we started? If there's one parallel world, I'd guess there's an infinite number of them. We might wind up where Hitler won or the bubonic plague wiped out the human race."

"So we're stuck?" Brad nodded. "But what do we *do?* We can't just stay on as permanent guests of Quintus Cornelius surely."

"It's not so bad here." Brad stretched. "Plenty of activities. And Quintus Cornelius wants us to talk with his bishop—the Bishop of London. He's at some conference in Rome, or rather on his way back from it. He's due in London—Londinium, that is—quite soon."

"And we're to tell *him* we come from a parallel world? Are you sure he won't decide to have us burned as witches, or warlocks, or whatever?"

"That's another way these Christians are different from ours. They've never got around to burning people. Quintus Cornelius doesn't think there'll be any theological hassle anyway. Multiple worlds isn't like multiple gods."

There was a sound of footsteps approaching, light on the tiled floor. Brad got to his feet, and Simon followed suit.

As he had guessed from the footsteps, it was a girl who came towards them. She was in her early teens and wore a tunic of what looked like white silk, the top gathered in folds on her shoulders and secured with a gold brooch. She had a thin gold chain round her waist and gold-painted sandals.

Brad spoke to her in Latin too fast for Simon to follow, and she answered him, smiling. She was black-haired, grey-eyed, and when she smiled, Simon realized how pretty she was. He also understood why Brad had been so quick to respond to the sound of her footsteps and why he seemed so content about being here. Brad turned to him.

"Simon, this is Lavinia—Quintus Cornelius's grand-daughter."

VI

THE MORE SIMON SAW of Quintus Cornelius, the more he liked him. He was a Christian but also, Simon learned, a proud Roman. His family, the Cornelians, was very ancient, with a pedigree going back two thousand years to the days of the Republic; he showed Simon ornaments, in a glass case, that had been worn by one of his early ancestors in a Roman triumph. He was proud, too, of the family's long history in the province of Britannia; they had lived here for nearly a thousand years, since another ancestor had come as governor. It was he who had been converted to Christianity and had to resign from office and give up senatorial rank. His descendants had stayed on in Britain after him, quietly and comfortably farming their lands. Nine hundred years seemed more like ninety, the way he spoke of it.

His pride was simple and impersonal, centred on the

past rather than the present. But there was one exception to that—his granddaughter, Lavinia. He had had one son, who had died of plague three years after Lavinia's mother died in childbirth. Lavinia had been more his child than his grandchild. Every look he gave her showed how besotted with her he was.

Simon could understand why. *Pretty* was an altogether inadequate term to describe her. The attractiveness of her features—the small, straight nose and big grey eyes, the thick black hair which always seemed to carry lights in it, the pale skin blooming to rose—was much less important than their animation. She smiled easily and devastatingly. And yet in repose her face had a distant look, as though she had sight of something far-off and wonderful, a dream landscape known only to her.

The boys intrigued her, but Simon was not sure she believed the account of their world and the crossing through into this one. She was continuously thinking up questions about the place they had come from and greeted the answers with incredulous laughter. A carriage, which moved along without a horse, on wheels filled with air, at six times the speed of a four-horse chariot? Pictures which travelled invisibly through the air, for thousands of miles, and then came to life again on the wall? But it was nice hearing her laugh.

Less nice, though, to have to sit in silence while Brad rattled on in what seemed like perfect Latin. Most of the time Simon could get only the drift of what was being said. But he had a bright idea about that. He explained how frustrating it was, and she agreed to give him lessons in the language. It was Brad's turn to look fed up. He attempted to join in but Lavinia would have none of it;

one teacher was better than two. Simon fervently agreed.

The other direction in which he scored was riding. Lavinia, as a Roman lady, did not ride herself, but she came out to the paddock at the far end of the garden to watch the boys. Brad had been learning with the help of a groom and was coming on well for a beginner. Simon, though, had the advantage of several years at a riding school, and even the unpleasant discovery that the stirrup was something this world had not got round to developing did not hold him back for long. He was soon exercising a fairly spirited horse while Brad plodded round on a placid hack. Lavinia was impressed and said so.

Simon had been at the villa for ten days when the Bishop visited them. He arrived on a blustery morning, with grey clouds trailing occasional stinging showers along the valley, without prior notice. The boys were told by the chief steward, Mandarus, to attend Quintus Cornelius and Bishop Stephanus in the *tablinum*.

"Tidy yourselves up," Mandarus said. He was a large calm, observant man, as much a friend to Quintus Cornelius as a servant. "It's a great honour, having a visit from His Holiness."

The *tablinum* opened out of the *impluvium* and was a sort of combined study and library. It was Quintus Cornelius's sanctum, and Simon had not been there before. The two men were talking together, side by side at the table, when the boys were shown in and stood respectfully by the door. The Bishop held his hand out, and Brad and Simon did as Mandarus had instructed them and went forward to kneel and kiss the ring with the big carbuncle stone. The other hand moved above their heads in blessing.

The Bishop was nothing like Simon's expectation. He had imagined someone very old—older than Quintus Cornelius probably—venerable and . . . holy-looking. Bishop Stephanus had a face that was deeply lined, but Simon thought he was probably no more than about forty; he had a curly chestnut beard without a fleck of white, and the hand was not an old hand. His movements and gestures were vigorous, and the gaze he directed on them when they stood up was keen. It was the look of someone used to command.

His voice was deep and seemed harsh, but after a few minutes Simon did not notice the harshness. He was too preoccupied with understanding and answering the fusillade of questions the Bishop proceeded to put to them both. He thought of asking him to slow down a bit, but didn't have the nerve.

He gradually worked out that the Bishop was testing the possibility that Quintus Cornelius might have been taken in by a couple of plausible young rogues. His rapid alternation of questions from one to the other and back was his way of finding out if they had combined to make up their story. He was banking on the possibility that if they had, one of them would get confused and give the game away. And he would have been right, Simon thought, as the interrogation finally and abruptly came to an end and he was able to relax into an exhausted silence.

The silence in turn seemed to last a long time. The Bishop ended it by turning to Quintus Cornelius.

"This is indeed interesting, Quintus. You were right to bring it to my attention."

He looked at the boys again. His face had no particular expression, but it made Simon feel weird. He felt as though if the Bishop had said, "Lie down—I want a footstool," he would have done so and even been glad to do it. It was the eyes, he thought. He wanted to look away, but could not.

"You tell a strange story," the Bishop said. "Of a world filled with wonders almost beyond imagining. Huge ships that cross the seas with neither sails nor oars. Others that ride the air like eagles, but big enough to carry hundreds of men and women. Or to carry death for hundreds of thousands."

His hand moved, making the sign of the cross.

"A world, too, in which there is a bishop in Rome but no emperor. And yet in which the Church is divided, flock against flock, brother against brother. Such stories are not easy to believe. They sound like tales a madman might utter in his ravings. But there is this."

He took something from the pocket of his robe and held it up. Brad's watch.

"The tales could be fantasies, but this is real. In this world there are no craftsmen who could forge such a thing, could make such a glass and seal it to metal, and could cause these strange shapes to flicker behind the glass. So it seems you are neither mad nor impostors. You tell me it is a kind of clock, and that, too, is a confirmation. Impostors would not have said anything so ridiculous."

He paused. "You come, you say, from a world that has the same lands and seas as this, lives in the same instant of time, the same space, and yet is wholly different. That is a mystery, but the centre of our faith is a mystery, too—the mystery of God in man. And it is not for us to set bounds to God's infinite creation. He who made one world could make two—a million if He chose. But there

78

is another question, to do with your presence here. Do you come on God's mission, or the devil's?"

Brad said quickly: "We are Christians, too, Your Holiness."

"Christians you say, but from a world in which the Body of Christ, His Holy Church, is torn asunder. It could as well be the devil's kingdom."

Simon felt cold. He remembered Brad's assurance that the Christians here were gentle, peaceful people, but that had been before they met the Bishop.

The Bishop put a hand to his beard.

"It was a decree of the emperor Julian that free men should shave their faces, but that slaves might not. He did not name Christians slaves, but I have chosen that title. We may worship our Lord in private, but not proclaim Him in public. That is slavery. We may walk the streets, but not go in procession to celebrate our faith. That is slavery. And we have grown used to our fetters, which is the worst slavery of all."

He stared at the boys and then, disconcertingly, smiled, but the smile was not reassuring.

"That which can be used for good is counted good. At last God has sent a sign! A miracle brought you here, and God's wonders are not worked for nothing. Nor must they be wasted. This generation is blessed, but only if it seizes its blessing and uses it."

The Bishop brought his hands together with a smack. It was an unexpected gesture following the mystical harangue, and made Simon realize the Bishop might be a practical man as well as a visionary. He wondered why that made him even more uneasy.

"Hold yourselves ready. There must be both prayer and

preparation. But I would be worse than the man who buried his talent in the ground if I failed to use God's miracle in the service of His Church."

After the Bishop had gone, Simon did his best to forget him. The lessons with Lavinia continued; it was very agreeable to sit with her in the cool of the *impluvium* or stroll along the garden paths while she told him Latin words and phrases and corrected his mistakes. Being chided for mistakes was pleasant, too, the way she did it. Brad made an attempt to join the class, but Lavinia told him he spoke Latin well enough already. He looked less than delighted with the tribute and suggested the lesson had gone on long enough anyway—couldn't they go and do something outdoors?

Lavinia said: "You go, Bradus. Simonus still has a lot to learn."

Simon said: "Yes, Bradus, you go." He said to Lavinia: "I'm sorry to be so stupid."

"You must think harder."

She smiled, though. Simon said earnestly: "I will."

Brad looked disgusted and walked away, but not far. He moved pieces on something like a chessboard. It wasn't chess but *Latrunculi:* a war game in which you had three sorts of pieces—pawns, rangers, and guards—to attack your opponent's base and protect your own. It completely baffled Simon, but Brad had mastered the rules and played games against Quintus Cornelius in the evenings. At the moment, Simon thought, his heart was not in it.

Lavinia's scolding of Simon's inability to remember simple expressions in Latin balanced neatly with her admiration of his skill on horseback. Brad cast around for something which might even the score and came up with log wrestling.

It was called that and had perhaps originally involved wrestling on an actual log, but in its present form a plank about two feet across was used. It required a combination of wrestling and balancing skills and was not as easy as it seemed.

The villa had its own bathhouse, heated by a subterranean furnace which in the cold months also supplied under-floor central heating to warm the villa. The bathhouse stood adjacent to the villa, and next to it was the *palaestra*, the exercise yard. Simon and Brad wrestled there, on planks fixed a few feet off the ground.

At the beginning Simon won fairly consistently, through superior weight. But Brad persisted and gradually developed a skill which, coupled with his greater agility, made the contests more equal. They began to take turns in toppling or being toppled into the dust, to applause from Lavinia.

Simon began to get bored with this and was pleased when Brad suggested one morning that instead of going to the *palaestra*, they should stroll down to the river. It was a grey day, but warm, and despite the lack of sunshine, bees hovered over the roses as they made their way through the paths and levels of the formal garden. The buzz of bees was always to be heard: with honey the only sweetener, they formed a vital part of life at the villa. They went on through the kitchen garden, where servants worked under the bidding of the head gardener, and down to the river.

It was about a dozen feet across, fast-flowing and fairly deep. On the far side, an artificial grove provided a background to a lawn with a summerhouse. There were two bridges. One was broad and sturdy and had handrails; an older construction was much narrower, and if it had ever had handrails, they had gone, perhaps to be used in building the other. Part of the bridge itself was missing, too; it was several feet wide at either end but shrank to not much more than a foot in the centre.

Brad was in the lead. He ran onto the old bridge, crossed quickly, and looked back. He called: "We missed our bout this morning. How about this?"

He came back until he was standing on the narrow section and adopted a wrestler's crouch. Simon realized two things. One was that this had been planned in advance. The other was that his chance of emerging the winner was not very bright. Forgetting the river (if one could), the bridge was at least three times as high as the planks in the *palaestra,* and he did not have a good head for heights. He could remember mentioning that to Brad, soon after they met, in the course of a discussion about Niagara Falls. Brad, plainly, had filed that, too, in his remarkable memory and was now ready to take advantage of it.

While he was hesitating, Brad called again: "Want me to stand on one leg?"

Lavinia beside him gave a small gurgle of laughter, probably only at the sight of Brad's antics, but it sharpened Simon's awareness of his predicament. He had a choice between refusing the challenge and looking chicken, or accepting and being made to look a fool. He glanced down at the river. A wet fool, too.

Brad said: "That's all right. I'll fish you out."

Simon advanced. He didn't look down again but was very conscious of the drop and the rushing water. Brad crouched, waiting. Simon dropped into a matching crouch, but only for a moment. He straightened up and ran at Brad, sweeping round with his right arm just before they made contact. There was no wrestling: just impact and the pair of them falling. He tightened his hold as they hit water, bearing Brad down till they struck the pebbled bottom. Then he let go. As he came up, he saw Lavinia above him on the bank; she looked concerned till Brad surfaced in turn a couple of yards away. Simon grinned at her, and she smiled back.

He struck out for the nearest reasonable landing, a little downstream. He had almost reached it when his right leg was seized, then his left, and with a twist Brad pulled him under. As they struggled, Simon was disconcerted to find that Brad was a stronger swimmer and that his own weight advantage no longer helped. He went down, struggled to the surface, and was dunked again. The third time he got a mouthful of water instead of air. When Brad finally permitted him to get to the bank, he was choking and gasping in a very undignified fashion. Lavinia was laughing uncontrollably.

The good news came next morning when they were called into the *tablinum*. Word had come from Londinium. The Bishop wished to examine Brad at greater length; he was to go to him at once.

Brad asked: "For how long, sir?"

Quintus Cornelius shook his head. "It was not stated. But for a long time, I think—weeks, perhaps. I shall miss our games, Bradus."

"And Simonus—what about him?"

"He was not asked for." Quintus Cornelius looked at Simon in commiseration. "I am sorry His Holiness cannot find a use for you at present, but . . ."

Simon said cheerfully: "That's all right, sir. It's Bradus

who knows it all. He'll be much more use than I could be."

— They saw Brad off in the *cisium*, a light two-wheeled gig which would convey him swiftly to the city and the Bishop. Lavinia said: "We shall miss you, Bradus."

Brad was doing his best to look unconcerned. Simon thought cheerfully of the difference in their prospects. For Brad, long, grinding hours of interrogation, punctuated by religious harangues. For himself, the easy life of the villa, with nothing to do but amuse himself. And Lavinia. Echoing her, he said solemnly: "Yes, we shall miss you, Bradus." He grinned and added in English: "But don't hurry back on our account."

The driver cracked his whip, and the gig set off at a brisk pace. Simon turned to Lavinia: "You said you might read some poetry to me, in the summerhouse. That sounds like a good idea."

VII

IT WAS NICE WHILE IT LASTED, but it didn't last long. Four days later, Simon was summoned to the *tablinum* again. There had been another message from the Bishop: He wanted him as well.

Simon attempted to argue. "But I wouldn't be of any value to him. There's nothing I know which Bradus doesn't know better. He has a fantastic memory—he can remember everything he's ever read. Whereas mine's terrible."

"That may be true, Simonus." A pause provided a moment of hope. "But His Holiness requests you, and that is enough."

He spoke calmly but with authority. And in this world, Simon remembered, authority did not tolerate opposition. That didn't just apply to slaves and the female sex. A son, for instance, was under the absolute power of his father, to the extent that even after he was married, he could not possess anything in his own right; he lived on an allowance, conditionally on behaving himself. And if instant obedience was required of a son, how much more so in the case of someone like himself?

He bowed. "When am I to leave, sir?"

"Immediately," Quintus Cornelius said, "of course."

He did manage to get a few minutes alone with Lavinia. She put her hand in his. He squeezed it and was delighted when she very slightly responded. He said confidently: "I'll be back soon."

"I hope so. But Bradus has not come back, and Grandfather thinks he may not for a long time."

"It's different with Bradus."

The difference being, he reflected, that while Brad might have the edge where academic knowledge was concerned, cunning was something else again. The Bishop had presumably called for him in the hope that he might know something more than he was getting from Brad. He had worked out an effective way of dealing with that. He had, he knew, put up a poor show in comparison with Brad at the previous interview; that would be why the Bishop had asked just for Brad in the first place. Confusion from the Bishop's rapid-fire questioning, made worse by his inadequate Latin, had had a lot to do with it. He reckoned that with a little thought he could appear dumber still. A couple of days of well-meaning stupidity, and His Holiness would be glad to be rid of him.

He asked: "Will you miss me?"

A small nod. "Yes."

"Truly?"

She looked at him. "Yes, Simonus, truly."

A sharp look round showed they were free from observation. He quickly bent down and kissed her. It landed high up on her cheek, and she immediately pulled away. But she did not look upset.

On the journey out to the villa Simon had been too preoccupied with talking to Brad to take in much of his surroundings. In the *cisium*, sitting beside a taciturn driver, he could observe things better. The approach to Londinium was something of a sprawl, with rows of hovels crowded alongside the road for half a mile before they reached the gate.

It was a very old gate. The brickwork was crumbling in several places, and the heavy wooden doors looked as though they had not been closed for centuries. On one side, in fact, a small hut to house the sentry had been built against the door, and would have to be demolished before it could be closed. The sentry was on duty but made no challenge as the *cisium* rattled through. And beyond a couple of feet on either side, the wall was invisible beneath the clutter of buildings clinging to it. Plainly it was meant as no more than a token defence, as one might expect in a land that had been at peace for more than a thousand years.

Inside, there was a further stretch of mean-looking buildings before they came to shops and larger edifices. The shopfronts were on the pattern he had seen before, but some had translucent glass windows, and some were double-tiered with staircases leading up from the street. There was the usual bustle of activity—vendors crying their wares, beggars calling, sometimes yelling, for alms— and a constantly changing mixture of smells: fruit and flowers, fish and cooked meats, leather and liquor, and the nauseating whiff of drains.

The buildings became still more impressive as they approached what Simon realized must be the quarter of the forum. The road broadened, and they clopped past large houses with only their roofs showing behind high walls, temples with porticoed entrances above flights of marble steps, the massive outline of the baths, and the great curving arc that was the circus. It would be deserted now. He remembered the gale of voices roaring for blood.

It puzzled him that the streets started getting meaner again. The driver halted the *cisium* in a street of shabby buildings and indicated that he should descend. He led the way through a narrow tunnel into a courtyard and left him there. The place was no more impressive inside than out. He realized he had been expecting the Bishop to live in something like Lambeth Palace, with a Roman version of Westminster Abbey close by. The driver came back with Brad and left them together.

Simon gestured towards the buildings.

"Not quite what I imagined."

"The Christians are poor relations on this side, remember."

"I wouldn't describe Quintus Cornelius as a poor relation."

"It's OK for individual Christians to be rich, but the Church has to keep a humble profile." Brad paused. "How's everything at the villa?"

"Fine."

"And Lavinia?"

"She's OK."

He had spoken shortly. Brad grinned.

"Parting is such sweet sorrow—that right?"

He made no reply, and Brad led the way into one of the buildings and up a stone staircase. They went along a landing painted with Christian murals to a small room overlooking the courtyard. It was sparsely furnished, but the walls were thick with religious paintings, and there was a bronze crucifix in one corner. Brad said: "Our sitting room. Privilege of special guests."

Simon said: "I've seen worse. I don't suppose I shall be here long."

"No? How do you figure that?"

Simon shrugged. "You're the one with the brain and the information. I shouldn't think the Bishop would need more than half an hour to pick mine clean."

"Such modesty." It was mock respectful, and Brad was grinning. "Come on. Time for *prandium*. But I hope you've not worked up too big an appetite. It's not like life at the villa. They go in for modest eating here as well. You'll need to tighten your belt a notch for that half hour you're going to be around."

The Bishop's study was small and bare, too, but it had a much bigger crucifix with a broad halo that looked like real gold. The Bishop was writing on a wax tablet and continued for some moments before looking up.

"Be seated, Brother Simonus."

Brother carried a suggestion of belonging Simon did not much care for. The aim, he reminded himself, was to be stupid, but not too stupid. Confused, more—sounding as though he wanted to be helpful, but totally useless.

"As a Christian you are already bound in service to the Church. But the enterprise ahead of us is no common one. Raise your hand. Swear, in Christ's name, that you will keep secret all you learn here."

He mumbled what was required. The Bishop's eye fixed him.

"Keep your oath, or meet God's judgement."

As soon that, he thought, as the Bishop's. He listened as the Bishop started explaining just what the enterprise was. He found considerable difficulty in grasping it, but the difficulty was not so much in the language as psychological.

In the past few months he had come to a view of the Roman Empire almost indistinguishable from those whose ancestors had been part of it for more than sixty generations. Its power was unshakeable, its permanence eternal—or as good as. It required qute an effort to appreciate that what the Bishop had in mind was a revolt, aimed at overthrowing the Roman army, the emperor, and Rome itself.

The fireball was the root of the matter. It was, in the Bishop's view, either the Holy Ghost or a very senior angel, and it had brought them to be the means of enabling the followers of the Lord to destroy the slaves of false gods. They—Bradus and Simonus—were chosen instruments of the divine will.

The Bishop's eyes, fixed on his, made it unnecessary to pretend confusion.

"Your Holiness . . . I do want to help, I mean, of course I do . . . but . . . it's Bradus who can help you . . . with information. . . . I mean, I don't really know anything . . . anything useful . . . anything he wouldn't. . . ."

The Bishop let him stutter into silence, then said: "That is true, Simonus."

He suppressed a sigh of relief. But the Bishop went on: "You have a part to play, all the same. God is with us, but the Roman soldiers have been trained in the use of arms. It will not be easy for men unused to fighting to overcome them. But there are others who have acquired skill as warriors—those condemned to fight and die for the amusement of the godless. The gladiators. By the Lord's will you shared their servitude, and came to know a man called Bos, who is both Christian and gladiator. He is the one who must persuade his fellows, Christian and non-Christian alike, to rise at the appointed time. And you, Brother Simonus, will be our messenger to him."

Brad asked: "How did it go, Brother Simonus?"

Simon stared at him. "I've been working something out."

"You have? Something good, I'll bet. Go ahead—I'm listening hard."

"When the Bishop was at the villa, I never said anything about being a gladiator."

"But someone told him? Quintus Cornelius, maybe?"

"Maybe. But Quintus Cornelius didn't tell him about Bos because he didn't know. Only one person knew that."

"Well, now! Those stories about the English being dumb—I never did believe them. Not altogether anyway."

"I think it might be an idea if I finished what I started, before the fireball, and beat you to a pulp."

Brad laughed. "You could try. Might look peculiar, though, in an instrument of the divine will? Think it'll get you back with Lavinia?"

Simon weighed the satisfaction of thumping Brad against the possibility of there being something in what he said. He undoubled his fist. Some things improved with waiting.

He said: "OK. We'll leave it till this lunatic business is over. That ought not to be too long."

Brad kept a wary eye on him. "You think it's lunatic?"

"Planning to overthrow an empire that's lasted two thousand years? What would you call it?"

"Everything comes to an end some time. There's no more magic in two thousand years than two hundred. Julian did a good job stabilizing things, but there's no way you can build a system that gets rid of all resentments. The Christians stopped martyring themselves when he dropped the religious oath of allegiance, but that didn't mean they were happy. A fuse being long and slow doesn't make the explosion any less violent."

"So what? One legion could put down the Bishop's crazy revolt. A single cohort could! And there are three legions in Britain and another four just across the Channel, in Gaul. What else but lunatic?"

Brad leaned against the window ledge. It was the eleventh hour, and the sky was darkening behind him.

"The Bishop is a pretty remarkable man," he said.

"Maybe. But he'd need to be more than remarkable to take on the Roman army."

Brad shook his head thoughtfully. "It didn't take long to work out what he wanted from me. He's well aware what chance a revolt against the Romans would have under normal conditions. The only way of reversing the odds would be to bring in some devastating new weapon. This world has seen nothing new in that line for over twenty centuries. It's very different in the world we came from."

"What does he want you to do," Simon asked, "—build him an H-bomb?"

Brad grinned. "That's something I never did read up on. I guess the basic technology would take awhile to develop; and the Romans might get curious if they saw something like Oak Ridge going up. My idea was gunpowder. Mortars, cannon, primitive rifles. I could have helped him there."

"But you didn't?"

"He didn't want it. It would still take too long. The Bishop wants faster action."

Simon was curious. "What, then?"

"We went through the history of warfare in our world. We picked two technical developments which switched the odds and guaranteed victory for the side that had them."

"Which were?"

"The stirrup and the longbow. The stirrup was introduced in the eighth century and made the Frankish cavalry the masters of northern Europe. Before that cavalry meant only what it still means here: a way of getting soldiers to the scene of the action quickly. They have to dismount to fight.

"Five hundred years later, Edward the First came up with the longbow, and at Crécy and Agincourt those conquering horsemen got themselves massacred. The longbow stayed dominant for more than two hundred years—until the invention of firearms, in fact. Either one could do the trick probably, against an army which has spent centuries rehearsing stale tactics, with no real fighting. The Bishop plans to make sure by using both. Both are simple to make and to learn to use. You don't need factories or complicated machinery. That's what I mean by remarkable."

Simon shook his head. "I still think it's crazy." He paused. "If it could happen, would you be in favour?"

"I haven't been asked. But I think I might. This place is overdue for a change."

"I don't see much wrong with the way things are."

"No? With worldwide ignorance—organized brutality like the Games? And how about slavery? Have you forgotten what it's like to squat in the dust, wearing nothing but a length of rope? Or is slavery OK now that it doesn't apply to you?"

Simon ignored the questions. He really didn't care what happened with the Bishop's revolt. The important thing was getting back to the villa, and Lavinia. And probably the best hope of achieving that was to do what the Bishop said, for the time being, at any rate.

Simon had been given instructions for locating the tavern, but he still didn't find it easily. It lay in the centre of a warren of dilapidated streets east of the barracks and was one of many—in some streets, branches of ivy seemed to hang from every roof. The ivy was the only thing to show wine was sold; there was nothing like an inn sign. But though his first choice was wrong, Bos was known there. He was directed to a place even more squalid in the next street.

A couple of men were drinking from battered metal pots. Simon found an empty pot and rapped with it on the stone counter. There was a shuffle of feet beyond a narrow doorway, and a woman came through. She had to turn sideways slightly; she wasn't tall, but she must have weighed close to two hundred pounds.

She looked at him suspiciously; her face was round, but not soft. He asked for Bos, and after a long stare she called into the back room for him.

Could this be the girlfriend of whom Bos had spoken with such affection? Bos himself provided confirmation by entering and giving the woman a loving pat that set the mass of flesh quivering. Then he said, shaking his big head in amazement: "Simonus! Is it you?"

Simon put a hand out, but it was disregarded; he was embraced and felt his ribs creak. Then Bos stood back and looked at him with concern. He touched Simon's shaven chin and, with a quick glance towards the two men, pushed him through to the back room. It was mainly furnished with kegs, but there were a couple of chairs. In a troubled voice, Bos said: "Running away is bad enough, Simonus. But to pass yourself off as a freedman . . . It means the beasts."

"I have been freed." Bos regarded him suspiciously. "And I've come here as a messenger. From His Holiness the Bishop."

"The Bishop?"

Bos shook his head again. Simon had been told to administer the oath of secrecy, and he decided to get it over with. He felt like a fool doing it, but Bos took it seriously. And it seemed to remove any doubts he had. He listened solemnly as Simon began to explain what was required.

He was almost immediately interrupted by a girl appearing in another doorway, but Bos barked a dismissal which sent her scurrying off.

"Macara's sister," he explained. "Go on, Simonus."

Macara must be the fat one, which meant that this was the girl Bos had had in mind for him. Thinner, certainly, but with lank, greasy hair, a sallow skin, and a mouthful of bad teeth.

He stated the case as plainly as possible, simply saying that the Bishop was planning a holy war against Rome, that he had new weapons which would overcome the legions, and that Bos's mission was to win over the gladiators to be the spearhead of the rebellion.

It sounded thin and unconvincing, an invitation to disaster. Bos, whose profession was fighting, would surely see that. For that matter, why should someone who so far had uncomplainingly accepted everything that fate sent his way turn rebel anyway? He waited for the slow, judicious headshake he had grown familiar with during the long days of training as a *secutor*.

But all Bos said was: "His Holiness has greatly honoured me. It will be done."

He was a Christian, of course. Loyalty to his Church could outweigh professional reservations. He was, too, a man accustomed to facing death and long odds.

Simon said warningly: "You're to win over all the gladiators—not just the handful of Christians."

The big face broke into a grin.

"Leave it to me, Simonus!"

VIII

ALTHOUGH UNIMPRESSIVE as a building, the Bishop's headquarters was extensive; it took up an entire block of small dwellings linked by a maze of alleys and yards. At the heart was the chapel, the one place richly decorated. The walls were painted gold, and rounded corners gave you a feeling of being inside a big golden egg.

It was a feeling Simon had plenty of opportunity to experience. There was Mass twice daily, and you needed a better excuse than he could think up to be absent. Morning Mass, though it involved unpleasantly early rising, was at least fairly brief, lasting not much more than an hour. (An hour, at this season, was approximately sixty minutes, though since the Roman day was divided into twelve equal parts, it would get shorter with the approach of winter.) In evening Mass, though, the interminable succession of psalms and hymns and Scripture readings dragged on for nearly three hours. He drowsed through it, watching the flickering candles and thinking of more attractive things—usually Lavinia.

The remainder of the day was not much less boring. Brad spent a lot of time with the Bishop, but Simon was left to kick his heels. There was no prospect, it was made clear, of his returning to the country. On the other hand, there was no prohibition on going out into the streets, and he did that. It was more interesting, but there was one big drawback. The Christians presumably used money, since food was bought in the market, but no one seemed to think it necessary to provide him with any. The smells from the food shops—fresh-baked bread, hot pies, fried fish, meat stews—were tantalizing after the plain and meagre fare of the community, but the cheapest thing appeared to cost a couple of brass *sestertii*, and he didn't even have a copper *as*. He would have liked to visit one of the music-and-dance shows in the booths beside the forum, but they required money, too.

So he wandered aimlessly, watching people and looking at the buildings. The Temple of Julian was the most impressive, bigger even than the temples of Jupiter and Venus. It stood isolated, with traffic passing all round, approached by marble steps on each side. From the shadowy darkness beyond the columns at the top came the sound of chanting, and sacrificial smoke plumed into the sky. Its magnificence, compared with the poky Christian chapel, put the Bishop's wild ideas into proper perspective.

Autumn had come, bringing chill grey days with the wind blowing the dust or the sharp rain laying it. He had a *birrus Britannicus*, something like a duffle coat with a hood, but it was well worn, threadbare in places: poor protection against a northeaster. The wind was knifelike as he turned away from the temple and trudged back.

He found Brad packing and asked: "Going somewhere?"

"Yep." Brad's face was expressionless.

"Where?"

"The planning's over. From here on we're into armaments. I've got a foreman's job at last."

"Away from here?"

Brad shrugged. "Has to be. No room here to swing a *feles*, let along stockpile longbows."

Simon said nothing. The place was going to be even duller, he realized, without Brad. Brad said: "Don't you want to know where the factory's to be?"

He shook his head. "Not much."

"Has to be off the beaten track, to escape prying eyes. And within reach of a good supply of the right wood. So, would you believe, it turns out Quintus Cornelius has a plantation of yew trees on the other side of the valley from the villa. They make a special line of furniture from them."

Brad was smiling. "Anyone down there you'd like me to give regards to?"

The next day Simon was given another errand. Two prototype longbows had been made. Brad had taken one to the villa; the other was to be delivered to Bos. It was raining when he set out, the bow concealed in a bolt of cloth on his shoulder. There were few people about; anyone with any sense would stay indoors.

He was hoping for a rest at the tavern and a chance to

dry off a bit in front of a fire; but Bos was eager to try the weapon out, and they set off again at once. They slogged on through still meaner streets, in thickening rain, to a disused brickfield on the outskirts of the city. It was about a hundred yards long, surrounded by a broken-down wooden fence. Piles of bricks stood like islands in the mud, and a lean-to provided some shelter at one end. There Simon unwrapped the cloth and gave Bos the bow.

Bos said: "The Parthians use little ones, shooting them from horseback. I have seen them in the Games. But you could not fire this from a horse. You have arrows?"

"One."

He produced it. It had a tip of beaten iron, which Bos examined critically. Simon said: "You fire these standing. I'll show you."

He fitted the arrow to the string, drew it back, and let fly. It landed some fifty feet away. He said: "I'll get it back and try again."

"Leave it to me," Bos said.

He tentatively shook one of the timbers supporting the lean-to, then with a grunt uprooted it. It was about eight feet by two and a couple of inches thick. Bos carried it effortlessly about twice the distance Simon's arrow had travelled, and wedged it upright in a pile of bricks. He picked up the arrow on the way back.

Taking the bow from Simon, he flexed it experimentally. Simon's effort had scarcely bent the bow; in Bos's hands it gave like rubber.

Simon said: "The arrow's supposed to be capable of penetrating a breastplate."

Without answering, Bos fitted the arrow, took aim, and fired. Even the hiss through the air sounded different—a stabbing, purposeful snake instead of a feeble, listless one.

The arrow stuck quivering in the plank, and Bos and Simon went out to look. The head had gone through the plank as though it were cardboard, and stood inches clear on the other side. Bos nodded approval, shaking raindrops from his grizzled hair.

"A good weapon, but it wants learning. I aimed for his chest, and it went a foot over his head."

"All right for someone with your muscles," Simon said. "Mine wouldn't have scratched a bare chest."

"It will come with practice."

Bos twitched the arrow and broke the shaft close to the point of impact. He drew it through and gave both parts to Simon.

"Go back and tell His Holiness if he gives me fifty such weapons, I will find him fifty good right arms to use them."

Three weeks later the bows arrived and had to be delivered to the barracks. Simon and Bos joined forces at the tavern. It was a bright, cold day, with a wind that found the chinks in Simon's *birrus*. He felt a different kind of chill as they approached the grim façade he had first glimpsed stumbling through summer dust. If they were caught smuggling in weapons . . . He imagined he could hear the snarl of the lions.

Bos steered the donkey to the right-hand side of the archway and chatted amiably while the guard ran casual hands over the bundles tied to the donkey's flanks. With a final exchange of jests they were waved on through.

"Like I told you," Bos said. "Easy."

Simon released breath. "What if he'd decided to make a thorough inspection?"

"No question of that."

"You couldn't be sure."

"Sure enough!" Bos laughed. "Since he's one of us."

"A Christian? But he's a Roman soldier."

"No, not a Christian. Not yet anyway. But one of us as far as this little game is concerned."

After that Simon was not surprised to find that the clothing quartermaster, a thin dark man with a pointed beard and knowing eyes, was also in the conspiracy. The three of them stacked the bows and arrows, covering them with linen. He was impressed by what Bos had already achieved, but it reminded him of something he would have preferred to forget: that these were preparations for a real event. What Bos called a little game actually meant the launching of a handful of men against the might of Rome. Like Spartacus, another gladiator. He remembered how that story had ended, with three hundred crosses lining the Appian Way into Rome, a hundred years before the crucifixion of Christ.

On the way back they had a drink at the tavern. It was a dark red wine, almost black, and very strong. Imported from Iberia, Bos said. He wiped his mouth with the back of his hand.

"We shan't be drinking together for a while. Confined to barracks from tomorrow—getting ready for Julian's Games."

He had forgotten the gladiators' month of confinement before the Games. At least it meant preparations for the revolt would be held up. He said as much, but Bos winked.

"I can't get out, and you can't get in. But Roman soldiers can do both. Don't worry. Everything will go ahead."

He thought of saying that was not what he was worrying about—of urging Bos to drop the whole thing. But he knew it would be pointless; he could imagine the broad face creasing in bewilderment. It was he, after all, who had been the means of involving him.

They finished their wine and said farewell. The big man hugged him, and Simon hugged him back. Then he set off with the donkey through streets where lamps flickered in the gathering dusk.

There was news next morning which drove thoughts of Bos right out of Simon's head: He was to go back at once to the villa. He assumed this was because he was no longer of value as a contact with Bos, but discovered there was another reason on arriving there. A calvary squadron was being formed, under the command of Marcus Cornelius, a nephew of Quintus, and both he and Brad were included in it.

Simon disliked Marcus on sight. He was quite old, thirty at least, thin and very dark, with a classical Roman nose. His characteristic expression was a superior grin, but with little, in Simon's view, to be superior about. He had a high-pitched nasal voice which sharpened to a screech when he issued commands. He was stupid as well as complacent, frequently wrong but incapable of admitting or, for the most part, realizing it.

They exercised in open country further down the valley, practising formation riding and, more important, the mounted swordplay which the use of stirrups permitted. They rode against targets, slashing down wooden men. It was fun if you didn't think about the end in view. Or, of course, of your own part in that end. Simon had assumed their involvement in the Bishop's plans would be confined to the preparatory stage. It was an unpleasant shock to find they were expected to take part in the fighting. He said so as they trotted back from exercise.

Brad said: "You didn't really think the Bishop would pass up on anything he could use, did you? It's one of the things I admire about him. He's thorough."

"I should have thought he'd had enough out of us."

"Enough? This is for God, remember."

Simon was still resentful. "It's not our fight."

"Isn't it?"

"Not our world even."

"You still hoping the fireball will come back?"

"No, but . . ."

"Then it's our world."

"We don't have to get involved in changing it."

"No? You're being stodgy British again. And we've been through that." They were approaching the villa. "Anyway, if you don't like the heat, I guess you could always get out of the kitchen. No stockade, no guards." He grinned. "Someone might miss you, though. And I really don't mean me."

Being with Lavinia again certainly made up for a lot. She had volunteered to continue tutoring him, in the written language, and he had accepted with alacrity. There could be no question, at this season of the year, of using the summerhouse: they were obliged to sit in the *impluvium*, with servants and occasionally her grandfather passing through. The under-floor heating was in operation now, making the tiles warm to the touch. On clear days, air rose like steam from the open roof.

He tried to hold hands at first, but she drew away with a small shake of her head and a reproving smile. He guessed that was to do with the lack of privacy. He didn't know the ground rules for a young Roman lady who was also a Christian, but suspected they might be tricky. There were enough accidental contacts of hands or arms anyway, to make the lessons something to look forward to. And there was the additional satisfaction of knowing Brad to be out of the running. He seemed more interested in the coming revolt than in Lavinia, something Simon found very hard to understand.

Altogether, time passed quickly. It was with another unpleasant shock that he heard Brad say, as they rode up the valley one morning: "Only two more days to the real thing."

"It can't be so soon!"

"You've not been paying attention, have you? Too concerned with Latin grammar or whatever. Marcus told us it was scheduled for the opening of the Games of Julian and the People. They start nine days before the Ides, and that's the day after tomorrow."

He rode in silence, digesting the news. A gust of wind blew leaves across their path, and Brad's horse shied. He controlled it well; he'd turned into a good rider in recent weeks.

"No more Latin," Brad said. "And no more Lavinia. And off to the wars as well." His voice was infuriatingly cheerful. "It's a tough life, kiddo."

Lavinia suddenly proved elusive. Simon had known he would not see her that day because she was visiting an aunt, but he expected her to be back by nightfall. But a message came that her aunt was unwell, and she was staying the night with her. She still wasn't back when he returned from exercises next morning, and the afternoon of a dark, drizzling day went by with no sign of her.

The litter brought her back at dusk. Her grandfather asked interminable questions about her aunt's health, while Simon hovered beside them. The old man went at last, and Lavinia said she must go to her room, too, to dress for dinner.

He put his hand on her arm, and she looked at him.

"Please," he said. "Just a few moments."

They were in the *impluvium,* with lamps glowing warmly in niches on the walls and round the edge of the fishpond. She said: "What is it, Simonus?"

"You know we leave tomorrow, before dawn?" She nodded. "I don't know when I'll see you again."

"Perhaps you'll be back soon."

"When I do come back . . ."

There was a sound of footsteps. Words would have to wait. He kissed her, this time finding her mouth. She quickly pulled away, but she was smiling.

"I must dress." The footsteps were nearer. "Take care, Simonus. Come back soon."

THEY RODE TO LONDINIUM before first light, but stopped short of the city gate. They waited in the huts of a small Christian community, tethering their horses in the chapel.

Brad said: "I believe the local priest objected, but His Holiness overruled him. If the operation as a whole is dedicated to the glory of God, minor items of sacrilege can be overlooked."

They were eating a breakfast of bread and cold meat and wine. Simon said: "We're to make our move at the same time as the gladiators?" Brad nodded. "Which is when, exactly?"

"They're due in the circus at the beginning of the fourth hour, so they'll leave the barracks about two hours from now. Weapons will be on the supply cart. At the point nearest the forum they grab the guards, kill them, and head for the governor's palace. That's when we should be joining up with them."

"All timed by water clocks, so give or take a quarter hour. His Holiness never gave you back your watch?"

"Wouldn't help if he had. You need two for timing."

"Do you think you'll get it back after the glorious victory?"

"Maybe he'll have it mounted in gold and stick it on an altar. If we're instruments of the divine will, I suppose the same goes for our possessions. In fact, as far as the Bishop is concerned, everything comes into that category."

"If there is a glorious victory. If not, I suppose you can regard losing a watch as a very minor worry."

"I guess so."

There was silence. The air felt cold and oppressive. Simon put down his bread and meat.

"I don't think I can eat this."

"You ought to." Brad chewed on his own food for a moment, then put it down. "You're right, though. Sticks in my throat, too. Have a slug of wine."

Simon said thanks, and took the flask Brad passed him.

They cantered down the road two abreast, and as they came in sight of the gate, Marcus Cornelius ordered the gallop. Brad and Simon were six pairs back from the leader, with Brad on the left to take advantage of his left-handedness. Simon saw the Roman sentry emerge from the hut. His sword was scabbarded in his belt; he put a hand up as though to stifle a yawn. Then he stared in stupefaction at the advancing column.

He shouted something, but Marcus Cornelius was on

him, sword arm raised. The sentry cowered back, his arm now shielding his face. The sword flashed down, cleaving him at the shoulder. Blood, gouting from the collapsing body, sprayed Simon's leg as they galloped into the city.

Some people came into the streets to watch them, but the majority would have gone into the city centre for the procession and the Games. Rain began to fall out of the dead grey sky, spotting at first, but then more steadily. Ahead there was a faint dull roar of voices. They came into the broader streets, lined with the high-walled palaces of the rich. Simon saw a heavy gate being slammed into place; the mansions were being turned into fortresses, barring off their treasures from a suddenly dangerous world. The clatter of their hooves echoed back from the walls.

The tumult was nearer and louder. It was not the normal sound of a crowd but something wilder; it had fear and anger and triumph in it. But whose triumph? Suddenly they reached the scene of the fighting, with the shouting still somewhere ahead. Bodies lay terribly silent, some peaceful as though sleeping, others twisted in a final agony. Almost all wore Roman uniform.

Marcus Cornelius gave a roar—"Victory to God!"—and led them on in the direction of the shouting. The mob, howling beneath the steps of the governor's palace, parted for them. Simon saw figures of gladiators under the colonnade at the top, one with his fingers twined in the hair of a severed head. A gilded crown hung from its ear. He saw Bos, too, leaning on a sword, face split in a savage laugh.

Someone shouted that the remnants of the guard had fallen back to the Temple of Julian, and Marcus Cornelius whipped the troop off in that direction. He would be anxious to make up for having arrived late for the first battle; lack of courage was not one of his faults. They left the crowd cheering for Christus and the gladiators. The rain was coming down heavily, making the stones treacherous under the horses' hooves.

The streets by the temple were empty of all but a few, who scurried away as they approached. Shouting, Marcus Cornelius rode his horse up the steps. The steps were broadly pitched, but even so, it was crazy. It needed only one horse to go down and the magnificent charge would collapse in a ridiculous welter. Still, there was no choice but to follow.

Then, incredibly, they were at the top and riding through the colonnade into the temple. Daylight was faint behind them; ahead there was darkness apart from the glimmer of lamps on the walls and a flame flickering out of a hole before a marble altar. The altar was laden with gold ornaments, set with stones that sparkled in the flame's light.

The guards, plainly, were not here. Marcus Cornelius called a halt, his voice echoing eerily in the vaulted silence. A marble statue, twice life-size, stood behind the altar: It was the figure of a grave-faced old man wearing a golden chaplet and a laurel wreath. The god-emperor Julian. The air had a heady, pungent scent. Simon felt a fearful awe and had an idea he was not alone in that. No one spoke. The statue stared down at them as it had stared down on fifty generations of worshippers.

Footsteps broke the silence. A man came out of the shadows at the rear of the temple, dressed in white robes and carrying an ivory rod around which a golden serpent wound itself to display a fanged, hissing head at the top. His face was older even than the face on the statue, but

110

he walked with a steady tread. He was obliged to look up to Marcus Cornelius, mounted above him, but the look was one of authority, expecting obedience. In a deep, resonant voice, he said: "To come armed into the holy precinct is blasphemy. To bring in beasts not dedicated to the god is a worse sin. Begone, before the god strikes you down, into torments from which only death can offer deliverance."

The threat, delivered with that air of steely command, was chilling. Marcus Cornelius did not respond at once. The priest started to lift his rod; the golden snake looked live and venomous. Then with a shout—"Only Christ is God!"—Marcus Cornelius slammed down his sword, and the high priest fell across the altar. The cry echoed round them as blood spread over the marble.

"It was a good fight, Simonus," Bos said, "though short. A pity you came late. But there will be more fighting, God willing."

The last bit struck Simon as slightly odd, and whatever either God or Bos felt, the prospect didn't cheer him particularly. He confined himself to smiling.

Bos took another deep swallow of wine and bellowed for more. A servant girl came quickly, and took the empty jug. She was no longer a slave because the Bishop had declared all slaves free, but she cringed as the big man patted her.

"Good wine, this. Chian, they say." Bos stretched luxuriously. "Drinking Chian wine, in the governor's palace. Nothing wrong with that, eh, Simonus?"

It was a sentiment Simon felt he could more easily assent to. They were in the residential area of the palace, at the rear of the administrative section, looking out onto gardens which included a menagerie and a lake with a pleasure island in the middle. The lake reminded him of the one he had known in St James's Park, and he wondered if it could possibly be the same geographical location—if at this spot in that other universe Horse Guards might right now be clopping their way to the changing of the guard at Buckingham Palace. But no, they were quite close to the forum, and the ruins of the forum surely had been in the City. Not Horse Guards, then, but stockbrokers in bowler hats. The thought was even weirder.

The girl came back with the wine, receiving another pat from Bos. He offered wine to Simon, who shook his head; one glass was more than enough. Bos drank deeply, wiping his mouth with the back of his hand and his hand on an embroidered silk cushion. Outside, a pair of young fawns cropped the winter grass. Bos was getting drunk. He talked happily about the fight and how the guards had run like sheep.

He broke off as Brad arrived. He was a bit in awe of Brad. Simon he remembered as a fellow slave and pupil, but he associated Brad with people like the Bishop and the lofty Cornelian family.

Brad said to Simon: "I might have known I'd find you taking things easy."

"Any reason why not?"

Brad settled on a couch. "Better make the most of it. News has just come in. The Twenty-third is on the move."

Of the three legions in Britain, one was stationed in the far north, guarding the wall, and another at Deva (Chester). The Twenty-third at Venta Belgarum (Winchester) was responsible for the internal peace of the province, up to now a pretty soft option.

"How do they know?" Simon asked.

He had been on the point of adding "without tele-phones" when he realized that not only would it baffle Bos but also that he didn't have a Latin word to say it. *Telephone* came from Greek, so it wouldn't be *telephonus*. *Proculsonor?* Not that it mattered.

"Pigeon," Brad said. "From the local priest. His Holi-ness has quite an information network working for him."

"Will it tell him how to fight a legion?"

He was trying to work out a probable time. Winchester to London was—what? Sixty or seventy miles? On a good road a legion could probably make twenty-five miles a day. So in three days . . .

"Recruits are flooding in," Brad said.

"Not soldiers. Not gladiators either."

"Keen, though. And not only Christians. Original Christians, that is. Converts are coming hot and heavy to the god who won Londinium. And every woodyard in the city is busy turning out longbows."

"It was easy here. A small garrison, caught on the hop and soft from easy living. But a legion . . ."

"What's a legion," Bos demanded, "compared with the power of the Lord? The others were sheep. These'll be lambs for the slaughter. Bring them on!"

He brought his glass down heavily on the marble table, and it smashed into smithereens, except for the silver rim. Bos stared at the spilt wine and broken glass and burst into bellowing laughter.

The road ran arrow-straight beneath them, a long rib-bon of black cutting through green, south to Venta Bel-garum, north only a few miles to Londinium. They were somewhere in the inner suburbs of his London, in fact,

Simon thought. They were on a hillside, under cover of trees, with another hill opposite, and a small river running at this point close by the Roman road. Clapham? Brixton? He had no idea. There had been no rivers in the London suburbs he had known, but that only meant they had gone underground, part of the drainage system of the megalopolis.

The road had been empty except for an occasional *cisium* or lumbering wagon, but was empty no longer. It moved steadily towards them from the south: a single dark shadow at first, then a series of strips moving in unison. The stamp of feet provided a rhythmic base to the distant chorus of a marching song. The column stretched at least half a mile. Simon looked round at their tiny troop of horsemen. There was another newly recruited troop on the far side of the grove. There were the archers and foot soldiers concealed along the hillside. But altogether they numbered less than half of those approaching along the road. And *that* was a Roman legion.

At least he was mounted, providing him with a better chance of escape. Make for the villa, he thought . . . find Lavinia, and get her away. . . . He remembered what had happened after Boadicea's revolt was put down. Roman vengeance could be grim.

The head of the lead column was directly beneath their position. Simon could make out the words of the song they were singing; it was one he had heard the gladiators sing, each verse about a different girl. He wondered when the order to attack would be given, or if it would be. Marcus Cornelius, in command now of the whole Christian army, was on the hill opposite with the archers. The song ended, but the legion came on; the silence was broken only by the steady thump of feet and an occasional barked command. On and on it came, unflagging, relentless.

Simon did not hear the order. He saw the sky darken, turned from the winter afternoon's drab grey to a sudden blackness by the cloud springing out of the hill, soaring and falling. It fell on the marching column, shattering its solidity on the instant. They were individual figures that cried out in alarm and pain and fright, that fell or broke ranks. A second cloud struck, followed by a third. They did not know what was happening—how death could fall on them from out of the sky. And packed as they were, they provided an easy target even to unskilled archers.

While they were reeling, the foot soldiers rose from cover and attacked, shrieking battle cries. Galbus, a flaxen-haired man who had succeeded Marcus Cornelius in command of the cavalry troop, gave the order to mount. He set them at the charge against a group of Romans who had managed to form a defensive square. The others were shouting, and Simon found himself shouting along with them in battle lust. They drove into the square and through it. He slashed unthinkingly at the helmeted figures, heard men scream, and felt his horse stagger, with bodies beneath its hooves. They reined in beside the river, and he saw his sword dripping red. But the river itself was red, and thick with bodies like boulders. Behind them the foot soldiers were slaughtering the remnants of the square.

The news, and the revolution, spread like fire through a forest dry as tinder. At Deva, the commander of the legion tried to put down the people's rising. But the legion had been stationed there a long time; the faces in the

115

crowd in front of them were faces they knew, often faces of kinsmen. And the crowd called the name of the god who brought victory—greater than the great Julian, because he was his overthrower. The soldiers turned their swords instead on their commander.

Then they marched north, as the legion from the wall marched south. For three days they stood in lines, opposing one another, but day by day men slipped away from the legion of north to join the comrades who stood opposite them, and on the fourth day the legions came together, not in battle, but celebration.

All Britain paid allegiance to Christus, and to his servant, the Bishop.

THE BISHOP WAS NOT CONTENT with Britain. He at once gave orders for ships to be gathered from every port and assembled at Portus Dubris, where the sea crossing to the Continent was shortest. As soon as the fleet was assembled, the army, still growing, would march there and embark, to cross the straits.

Simon managed two visits to the villa before the marching orders came. On the first, Lavinia was away; on the second, although she was present, so was her aunt. Fabiana Cornelia proved to be a tall, matronly woman, her steel grey hair piled high in an elaborate coiffure, wearing a blue dress of stiff silk that looked more like steel. Lavinia was subdued in her presence, and Simon felt bothered under her cold scrutiny.

He was surprised when she said, just before he was due to leave: "I like your young barbarian, Quintus Ericius."

Ericius was Quintus's cognomen, a kind of nickname; it meant hedgehog, but no one seemed to know how it had originated. Quintus Cornelius put an arm on Simon's shoulder.

"Yes, he is coming on well. We shall make a Roman of him, I fancy."

Simon had a feeling Fabiana's opinion carried weight in family councils, and her unexpected words of approval made up to some extent for the fact that he did not succeed in getting a single moment alone with Lavinia.

He reflected, riding back to the city, that but for Lavinia, this might have been a good moment to go missing. Tomorrow the army moved south. This was not his war, and the prospect of helping carry it into Europe, against the full might of the imperial army, appealed to him even less. In the confusion that had followed the breakdown of central government and amid the subsequent sweeping changes, it ought not to be too difficult to find a new and safer identity. But of course, there *was* Lavinia, and deserting would knock out any hope of seeing her again.

The road passed between the hills from which they had ambushed the Twenty-third. The river ran clear over its stones, and the green slopes were empty and calm under a mild west wind and patchwork sky. The only sign of the happenings of a few weeks ago was the mass grave under the hill, surmounted by a wooden cross. The Bishop had ordered Christian burial for the enemy, even though they were pagans.

What mattered, Simon decided, was to make sure of coming back. The furious passion he had felt riding against the men of the legion seemed even more remote than the battle. Survival was the name of the only game that counted.

The mild spell continued as the fleet of ships set out from Dover harbour into a calm sea, with a small wind from the west. Bishop's weather, the men said. The air of general enthusiasm was infectious, but Simon avoided being infected by it. He said to Brad: "He's been lucky so far. That's the point."

"And he's taken advantage of the luck—which is what counts."

The horses, tethered in the well amidships, were being fed and watered by the grooms. Simon thought of the chaos a rough sea would have produced. He said: "The luck will turn eventually. It must."

Their ship was near the head of the formation; they could look out into empty waters. Simon said: "No sign of the imperial fleet yet."

"No sign of the Luftwaffe either. This isn't D day, with radio and radar and the whole bag of tricks. The emperor's not even had time to get spies into the province, let alone have them report back. I guess that's why His Holiness has moved so fast. He's got a general's instinct."

"Marcus Cornelius is supposed to be in command."

"That's right. And in another sense we're under the command of the Holy Ghost. But it's His Holiness who does the heavy thinking and the planning. Very well so far."

"Do you really think he can beat the emperor?"

Simon was aware of the change in his own attitude, in that he could even ask it as a serious question.

Brad shrugged. "Put it this way—I'd want good odds to bet against."

"And then?"

"Then?"

"What do you think is likely to happen if he does win?"

"Do you mean as far as we're concerned?" Simon nodded. Brad looked out to sea for some moments without answering. He said at last: "I've got one idea."

"What?"

"It'll wait."

He spoke with a finality which Simon knew would not easily be overcome. In any case, he was not particularly interested in Brad's idea, whatever it was. He had ideas of his own. He thought about them as the ship drove onwards.

The Christian army landed and pushed on south. There was no sign of an enemy. Instead, day by day there was an increasing buildup of recruits, and towns and villages opened gates and food stores to them. The triumphal receptions they were given meant that news of their approach had travelled ahead, which in turn meant that the imperial forces in Gaul must have been alerted to their progress. As the days passed, Simon began to find this ominous. The most probable explanation was that the opposing general was biding his time, luring them into the heart of Gaul so that he could not only destroy them but cut off their retreat. When they at last had sight of the enemy, he was sure that was it.

He did not know where they were, except that they were a long way south of the territory of the Parisi. Fairly flat country was starting to give way to land that rose in ridges towards high hills in the southeast. The imperial army was drawn up on high ground east of the road, with woods behind them.

It occupied several acres of ground. The front stretched for over a quarter of a mile, and it was nearly that in depth. The cohorts formed squares around a central tented area from which rose the smoke of campfires. A larger tent, presumably the general's, was decorated in purple and gold. The whole thing had a look of organization and efficiency, in marked contrast with the straggling Christian disorder. It was plainly far superior in numbers, too. Eagles that had been set up identified three legions: close to twenty thousand disciplined Roman soldiers.

This was towards the end of the afternoon, too late for there to be any fighting that day. The Christians camped on the other side of the road, about three-quarters of a mile from the enemy. It did not look like a particularly good position to Simon: on marshy ground under a hill to the south. But neither the conditions nor the awesome array of the legions seemed to dampen the spirits of the Christians; they sang hymns lustily as the moon rose in a clearing sky to the east. A chill white orb, almost at the full. A goddess Diana, in this world—not a dead cinder of a planet, littered with discarded space hardware.

They were still singing when the cavalry moved off; a local guide who volunteered to lead them round to a position in the rear of the legions had been found. Simon's irritation at having to start another trek when he had been hoping to bed down was balanced by satisfaction that they were moving out of the area that lay in what was likely to be the direct path of the legions' charge. He looked back as they led their horses, hooves muffled, round the side of the hill. Moonlight gleamed on quite large patches of water. They would be sliding in mud as well as blood tomorrow.

They travelled so far that he began to wonder if the guide had lost his way or was leading them astray. But apart from being dog-tired, he did not care much. Wherever they were heading, it was away from the killing ground.

A halt was called at last. They were among trees, but that was all he knew. He tethered his horse, wrapped himself in his cloak, and settled on the ground. There was moss underneath him. He tried to persuade himself that made it softer, without much effect. But tiredness provided its own featherbed; he fell asleep almost at once.

In the light of morning, they could see that they were behind and to the south of the legions, on higher ground and screened by trees. They could hear the sounds from the imperial army, but could not see them. But they had a clear view of the slope lower down, of the road, and of the Christian army beyond. They fed their horses on hay, themselves on hardtack of biscuit and dried beef, and waited.

It was a long wait. The sun stood high in the sky before they heard the trumpets blare their bristling defiance, and the familiar rhythmic stamp of feet began. It had the steady pulsating thrust of a steam hammer, making the earth vibrate under their feet. The legions which had conquered the world were on the move.

Further down the hill they came in sight: a long line of cohorts, followed by another, and another and another. The sky was a clear blue. Bishop's weather? But Sol Invictus was a Roman god, and his rays shone now on the massed brightness of shields and upraised swords. The front ranks came to the road, marched up the embankment, across, and down the other side without breaking step. It had more the look of a machine in motion than a body of marching men.

They moved in silence except for the stamp of feet. The Christians, who had earlier been singing hymns, had fallen silent, too. What did it feel like, Simon wondered, watching those lines of shields draw nearer? He was glad again he was not down there. The distance between the two sides steadily narrowed. Soon there would be the second trumpet blast that heralded the charge. But before that happened, unexpectedly there was movement on the Christian side. The narrowing gap widened again. The Bishop's army was retreating.

The trumpets sounded then, and the rhythm of the advancing feet changed, from march to jogging trot. They were going forward at the run, with water splashing up and catching the sunlight as they came to the marshy area. It was an impressive sight.

But as water splashed up, the dark hail came down: volley on volley of arrows from the bowmen on the ridge. The front ranks crumpled and broke, but the ranks behind pressed on blindly, with a terrible momentum. The cohorts crushed in on one another, blocking free movement. Men stumbled and fell, struggled to climb over bodies heaped beneath their feet, and still the arrows came. They stopped only when the Christian horde came howling back to throw themselves mercilessly on a demoralized rabble.

The rear guard, which had not yet reached the road, tried to organize itself to make a stand. That was when Galbus gave his order, and the cavalry swept along the hillside. The Romans stared in disbelief at the horses thundering towards them down the sunlit slope, then, before the cavalry even reached them, they broke and ran.

The Christians reached the sea at Massilia, which Simon worked out was Marseilles. The weather broke

123

simultaneously into storms of torrential rain, with occasional sleet or snow, and the army took up quarters in the port. The time was not wasted—there were new recruits to train and foraging parties to be sent out, not only for food, but for horses and wood that could be made into longbows. Where they could not find yew they brought in ash. The city's woodworkers toiled at their cumbersome pole lathes, and the harness makers made saddles and stirrups.

The troop of forty horsemen which had first surprised the Romans had grown to six troops by the time they moved on. Galbus had a wing of cavalry to command, and Brad and Simon had a new troop commander, called Curtius. He was a dark, stocky man, taciturn by nature. Simon at first thought him a poor exchange for the hearty, bustling Galbus, but Brad took a different view, and gradually Simon came to share it.

Curtius had an observant eye and a sharp, sardonic sense of humour. On rainy afternoons, when exercises were over, he took to joining Brad and Simon in a little wine bar on the seafront. Bos, who commanded the gladiators' company which was the spearhead of the foot soldiers, completed the quartet. Brad, though so much their junior and without military rank, seemed to do most of the talking. Simon had a feeling both men deferred to him a bit. That was sometimes irritating but, he told himself, unimportant. Before long the war would be over, and there would be better things to do than sit in a poky wine bar. He realized he no longer had any doubt of the outcome; he took the triumph of the Bishop for granted.

When the storms gave way to calm winter sunshine, the army set out again, refreshed and strengthened. They

124

took the easy road along the coast, north to a city whose name, Genua, had barely changed, then south into Italy. People flocked out to cheer them, and bunches of bright yellow mimosa were thrown in front of their horses' hooves. The Bishop also rode, but on a donkey, not a horse. Their progress was often halted by crowds wanting to be blessed by him.

There had, of course, to be resistance at some point; the emperor would scarcely surrender Rome without a fight. The final battle came at a place where the road, having gone inland from the coast, wound between small hills. The imperial army laid its ambush there.

Once again Brad and Simon had a spectator's view. The mounted forces were in the van, and the Romans let them through before launching their attack. They heard the trumpet blasts and looked back, to see dark lines of figures descending from the high ground on either side towards the main body of the Christians.

It was a classic operation, and under the conditions of warfare that had existed for more than two thousand years, the discipline of the imperial army would have guaranteed its success. But the Christian army was flanked along its length by bowmen, who sent their freight of death whistling into the charging lines long before they could get close enough even to throw their javelins. Simon had time to be amazed at the speed with which they fired and rearmed, producing that almost-continuous hail, before his troop was ordered into the attack.

The cavalry split, charging on either side of the road and striking the shattered Romans on their flanks. Their own cavalry, of course, used horses only for transport,

125

doing their actual fighting on foot. The sight of men riding down on them with upraised swords defied belief, but could not be denied. Coming on the heels of that distant hurling of death, it was too much.

The battle lasted little longer than the others had done, though some Romans did succeed in coming to grips with the main force of the Christians, and one small detachment broke through to where a black-crossed banner waved above the Bishop's head. Simon had a glimpse of the Bishop rising up from his donkey to smite someone with his crozier before more pressing matters engrossed him. What would happen, he wondered, if despite the victory the Bishop was struck down, as the emperor Julian had been in his world?

The speculation was irrelevant. It was soon over, with the black-robed figure still sitting his donkey, unscathed amid the carnage, praising God for His mercy.

The palace of the emperor, a marble miracle of pillars and porticoes, of terraces and arches and vaults and domes, was perched on the edge of the Capitoline Hill; from its widest terrace one looked out over the Forum and the whole city of Rome. The fate of the emperor himself was doubtful. Some reports had it that he had fled to the south and taken ship to Africa; others that he had been killed by his personal slaves, and his body thrown in the Tiber. At any rate Simon, together with Brad and Bos and Curtius, lay on his terrace, on couches decorated with gold, cushioned by silk and swansdown, and drank his imperial wine.

The Bishop's weather held still. Under the sky's blue dome the great edifices of the mother city gleamed in their different hues of marble—white and pink, red and ochre and pale green. In the parks trees slumbered with no stir of leaf, and fountains danced in the sunlight. Forum and streets were crowded, but neither noise nor emotions—whatever they might be—carried up here. All was peace.

Soon they would be travelling back to Britain; the Bishop had made it clear that having conquered Rome, he had no mind to stay there. Simon listened hazily to Brad talking, about a project he had in mind. He was fairly vague about it. The only thing that emerged was that it was some kind of expedition. Bos and Curtius appeared to be interested. Let them be, Simon thought comfortably.

He saw it first as a wisp of smoke curling up from the roof of the Temple of Julian and wondered about the fool-hardiness of whatever priests still tended the sacred fire. But the wisp thickened and darkened and, as he called to the others to look, sprouted pink flame.

Bos said: "Yonder, too. Look."

There must have been not one firing party, but several. One after another the temples turned to torches. They watched because there was nothing else to do, and the scene had a terrible beauty. From the temples the fire raisers turned to palaces and public buildings. As dusk fell, the flames were brighter still as they burned to ashes the ancient heart of Rome.

XI

THEY HAD TO WAIT ONLY three days for their interview with the Bishop. This was, as his secretary explained, an unusual favour; there was a six weeks' delay on the normal waiting list. Simon thought this encouraging, together with the fact that they were received in the same little room. Nothing had changed, either in the surroundings or the Bishop's own appearance. He wore the same small pectoral cross, not very well repaired at some time, the same worn robe and slippers. The intensity of gaze had not changed either. Simon was glad they had agreed that Brad should do the talking.

The Bishop said: "You seek a favour."

It was halfway between statement and question, unencouraging in tone. Brad said: "Not for ourselves, Your Holiness." The Bishop watched him in silence. "For a friend."

"State it."

"It's someone called Curtius Domitius. He commanded a troop of horse in your army—the troop Simonus and I were in. He served you well, Your Holiness. He fought in every battle through to Rome."

"Christ gives His rewards to faithful servants. I, a poor servant myself, have none to offer."

"Well, that's just it," Brad said. "Curtius isn't a Christian. As you know, a lot of those who fought on our side weren't. They joined us because they were opposed to things like slavery and the empire itself."

The Bishop nodded. "He has helped to liberate the Church. And the liberated Church liberates in turn and welcomes. Having been freed from false gods, he can follow the true God, through Jesus Christ, His only Son."

"Yes," Brad said. "I see that. But he doesn't want to."

A silence ensued. The Bishop showed no sign of wanting to end it. Finally Brad did.

"He's been told that as an officer in the army he's got to undergo the pendulum. He offered to resign, but he's been told that's not allowed."

In a bleak voice, the Bishop said: "These matters are the concern of others, not of me."

"But you could help," Brad said. "You only have to say a word to Marcus Cornelius."

There was another long pause, before the Bishop said coldly: "What word? To grant favour to one of our Lord's enemies?"

"But he's not! He just doesn't want to be baptized."

"Christ said: He that is not for me is against me."

Simon could no longer stay quiet. "Christ said a lot of things, didn't he? And nearly all of them were about

129

peace and loving one's fellowmen. Do you think he'd have approved of the pendulum?"

Immediately following the return from Rome, the pendulum had been set up in the high-ceilinged state room of the governor's palace, where it swung its murderous arc from wall to wall. Murderous, because its bob was a heavy cylinder of lead, with a sharp blade of iron set in on either side. An altar, surmounted by the figure of Christ, had been set up just in front of the point where the bob, at the lowest point in its arc, swept some four feet off the ground.

And at that point a small wooden enclosure had been built, big enough for a man but granting him only sufficient freedom of movement to be able to drop to his knees in front of the altar before the bob came down. Some of the more agile were able to sway their bodies just enough to have the bob miss them—on the first few swings anyway. Escape became continuously more difficult as the pendulum swung to and fro, and fatigue in the end made it impossible. The one time Brad and Simon had been there they had seen bystanders laughing and laying bets as to which would be the killing stroke, before they turned away, sickened.

Rumour had it that the pendulum had been devised by the Bishop himself—that the idea had come to him in a dream or vision. They had hoped that wasn't true; there were plenty of other ruthless fanatics about these days. But they had decided, anyway, to keep reference to the pendulum brief and unprovocative. As the Bishop's eyes burned into his, Simon had time to reflect that first thoughts had been best.

The Bishop spoke at last. "You are impertinent, Simonus. The devil, it is known, can quote Scripture. You would do well to remember that you no longer dwell in your old world of lawlessness and licence—that world in which any fool or knave feels free to mouth his corruption of the holy word—but in a world that has seen the triumph of divine truth, a world in which the Church, which is the Body of Christ, is one and indivisible, and victorious. Listen to your priests, both of you, and pray to God for deliverance from doubts and temptations." He gestured dismissal. "You may go now. The Lord go with you."

Outside, Simon said: "That wasn't too good."

"No."

"How long has Curtius got?"

"Before the pendulum? Days rather than weeks. The waiting list gets shorter all the time. There's getting to be quite a rush for baptism."

"Do you think *he* will—be baptized, that is?"

"Do you?"

One really only needed to put the question to know the answer. The Church might conceivably have talked Curtius into membership, but he would never be coerced into doing so, particularly when the coercion involved making him bend a naturally stiff neck.

"We could try again." Brad looked at him. "Maybe go to Marcus Cornelius instead."

"We *could* waste time doing that."

Brad was right—it was impossible to imagine Marcus Cornelius doing anything the Bishop might disapprove of—but the casual dismissal of the proposal was irritating. Simon said: "Do you have a better idea?"

"I might."

"Tell it then."

"Not right now. Let's go and find Curtius first. And Bos."

They sat in Bos's tavern, literally his now because with some of the gold they had brought back from Rome he had bought the freehold. He had brought some Frascati wine back, too, of a good vintage, and it filled a gold jug with a dolphin handle that once had served the emperor. Brad reported on the fiasco of their visit, and Bos growled angry comments. Curtius stayed silent, but looked stubborn. Simon had thought of trying to persuade him to be sensible and go through the ritual of baptism—it didn't mean anything unless you wanted it to, and you had only one neck—but he decided there would be little point.

Brad outlined another possibility: Curtius could flee from Londinium. They could fix it so that he had a couple of days' start before he was missed. But long term the chances were he would be picked up, and if not, he would be forced to spend the rest of his life as a fugitive. The Christians were in control everywhere, and it looked as though the persecution of pagans would only get worse.

They listened gloomily, Bos cracking the fingers of his large hands.

Brad said: "Obviously that's preferable to being put through the pendulum. But there's something else we can do. First I should say something about Simonus and me—about where we came from."

Simon looked up quickly; surely he wasn't going to talk about parallel worlds to Bos? Brad met his eye blandly. He said: "You know we come from across the sea. You thought it was one of the barbarian lands—the country of the Celts or the Norsemen. But it's neither of those. Ours is a great land—greater than Britain and Gaul and Spain and Italy and Africa put together—which lies far out in the western ocean."

Curtius stared at him with narrowed eyes.

Bos said: "There is no land in the western ocean, beyond the land of the Celts. Only the world's edge."

"We are from the land that lies at the world's edge. Isn't that so, Simonus?"

Simon could see now what was coming. The least he could do was nod.

Curtius said: "How did you get here? And why haven't others come before you?"

They were two good questions, but Brad dealt with them neatly. "The ocean is very wide. Wider than from here to Egypt, with no harbour for shelter in between. We were travelling from one part of our own coast to another, but our ship was blown off course in a storm. We lost both sails and rudder and drifted for weeks before she foundered. Simon and I took refuge on a raft, which cast us up, nearly dead from hunger and thirst, on the shore of Britain."

He said it convincingly. Bos was nodding, and Curtius looked more cheerful than he had done since their return to Londinium.

Brad went on: "With the gold we got in Rome we can buy a ship and sail it westwards. In our country there is peace, and men are free. No emperors and no bishops. No slavery and no pendulums. What do you say?"

"I am no sailor," Bos said. He grinned widely. "But I think I can learn!"

Curtius said slowly: "My father was a sea captain. If we could find a ship . . ."

"I've found one," Brad said. "She's lying here, at Londinium. She's twenty years old, but I've had her checked for seaworthiness. She worked the Africa run, so she's used to deep water."

Curtius said: "Then this is something you had in mind before you went to the Bishop?"

Brad nodded. "It would have been useful to have had more time. As it is, I guess we ought to move right away. We'll need to lay in provisions and stores, but I don't think we should do that here. Dubris would be safer."

Bos stood up. "I am ready now. Macara will be all right; she has the tavern and will find herself another man within a week." He clapped a hand on Simon's arm. "And by then, maybe, you will be showing me the wonders of this land of yours. It has women in it, I suppose?"

A week might just about see them clear of Land's End, but that was something for Brad to sort out.

Simon said: "Bradus will show you the wonders, Bos. I am staying here."

He hated saying it, but it had to be said right away. Curtius looked at him, suspicious again.

"If it is as good a land as Bradus says, why do you not wish to return to it?"

Brad intervened before he could answer. He said, with a grin: "What is there could make him choose not to go back to his own country? Only one thing, surely. He has found a girl he would rather stay with. Not so, Simonus?"

Simon nodded.

Bos said, puzzled: "I have a girl, too. What of that? There are girls everywhere."

"But you're older, Bos, and wiser! He'll learn in time. And when he has learned, perhaps he'll find another ship and come after us."

134

It hung in the balance for a moment; then Curtius relaxed and smiled.

Bos squeezed Simon's arm. "Soon, young Simonus. Grow up, and make it soon."

The usual feeling of excitement and anticipation was missing as Simon rode down to the villa. Thoughts of Lavinia were elbowed out of his mind by recollections of the others, particularly of the last time of seeing them, at the quayside.

She was called *Stella Africanus,* an impressive name for a less than impressive craft. She was not much above forty feet long, a minnow to the vessel tied up next to her, which was three times her length. But she could be handled by three men, Brad pointed out. Prow and stern were high, compared with the low section amidships where the mainmast was fixed, rigged for a mainsail and smaller topsails. In the bow a spar, canted steeply upwards, carried a small square sail. A sternpost featured a carving of a swan with a star on its breast.

He had cut the good-byes as short as possible, desperate to get away, and then had felt worse at the sight of Bos's puzzled, unhappy face. He had wished them luck, hearing the words come out cold and stiff. Brad had done his best to make light of it, saying they wished him luck, too, and capping it with a joke that brought a grin from Bos. Simon had walked quickly to where his horse was tethered and ridden away without looking back.

He visualized the ship in an Atlantic storm, with huge seas breaking over that matchstick mast. Curtius was the only one with any skill in seamanship, and that unpractised since boyhood. Brad had done some pleasure sailing off the coast of Maine, and Bos had the sort of hands that turned easily to most tasks, but it added up to desperate odds. They would be at sea now, beating south around the coast to Dover. He felt the wind in his face, fresh and from the west. They would have some tacking to do.

The sight of Lavinia helped. She came to greet him on the porch, with outstretched hands, wearing a dress he had not seen before, a tunic of shimmering grey silk which showed up the darker grey of her eyes. As he grasped her hands, he became aware of her grandfather approaching, too.

Quintus Cornelius was warmly welcoming. It was their first meeting since the return from Rome, and it was clear Simon had a new reputation as a conquering Christian warrior. Refreshments were brought, and they plied him with questions about his exploits. He answered with suitable modesty and was going well until Quintus Cornelius mentioned Brad, wanting to know why he had not come with him.

He ought to have expected the question, but it floored him. He stumbled his way through an answer: Bradus was busy . . . something for His Holiness . . . perhaps in a week or so . . .

Quintus Cornelius rescued him. "At least *you* have come, Simonus. And looking well after your adventures. You seem taller. Do you not think he looks well, Lavinia?"

She smiled. "Very well, indeed."

He had hoped Quintus Cornelius would retire and leave them alone, but the opposite happened; it was Lavinia who excused herself. There was an important dinner party that evening, and she had things to attend to. Quin-

136

tus Cornelius remained talking. He asked how things were in the city—he had not been there for some time—and Simon was emboldened to mention the persecutions.

Quintus Cornelius frowned. "Such things are not Roman. But bad things often happen in the wake of great events. This will not last, Simonus. His Holiness will see to it that all is put right."

It wouldn't do to point out that His Holiness was the prime persecutor. Simon remained silent as the old man went on: "Yes, we can leave all that to His Holiness. Let us consider *you*, Simonus. I said we should make a Roman of you, and I am proved right. There is your future to think of. Farming, perhaps, to begin with, but later you might go into politics. And there it is connections that count. It is a disadvantage that you have no family. But I think that disadvantage might be overcome."

He rose from his seat, smiling. "The Cornelian family is as good as any in the Roman Empire. Should one say that now? But whether or not there is an empire, the world is still Roman! And if at some point you were to find yourself a member of the Cornelian family . . ."

He pressed a hand on Simon's shoulder. "I must go now, Simonus. I will see you tonight at dinner. We have another victorious warrior coming. Our guest of honour is my nephew, Marcus, your commanding officer. I imagine you two will find things to talk about."

Dinner was at the ninth hour, and he didn't get hold of Lavinia again until shortly before that. She had changed into a white silk tunic trimmed with scarlet, and she had her hair up. She looked older and even more beautiful. They were in the corner of the *impluvium* next to the *tri-*

137

clinium, where servants were making final preparations for the meal, and he tried to draw her away to a spot where they could be more private.

She shook her head with a quick look in the direction of the servants, but let him keep hold of her hand. He was happy enough with that. There was a lot of time ahead, after all. Her grandfather's words came back, as they had done over and over again since they were spoken. "If at some point you were to find yourself a member of the Cornelian family . . ." How else except by, some day, marrying Quintus Cornelius's granddaughter? It was unbelievable, but it had been said.

So he contented himself with paying her compliments on her appearance. She said: "You look very fine yourself, Simonus. That's a handsome cloak."

It was a dinner cloak of blue satin, and he had already spent some time admiring it in the polished silver mirror in his bedroom. He said proudly: "Quintus Cornelius gave it to me."

She nodded, smiling. "He's very fond of you."

He wondered if he dared mention what had been said, but decided not.

In any case, she went on: "I must leave you, Simonus."

He protested: "I haven't had two minutes with you yet!"

"I know. But there are so many things to see to. Everything has to be perfect tonight, for our special guest."

"Marcus Cornelius?"

"Yes." In a deep voice, mimicking her grandfather, she said: "The commander of the Christian army."

"What a joke. The Bishop did the commanding—we all knew that. You know the Bishop rode a donkey to Rome?

138

That was the name the troops gave to the so-called commander. They called him Asinus Cornelius."

She laughed, but said in reproof: "Now, Simonus! I can't listen to you saying things like that about Marcus."

"I know he's your cousin, but he's still a pompous fool."

"And my future husband."

She was smiling, and after a moment he smiled back. "You almost had me believing you. I don't really think it's funny, though."

"It's not supposed to be funny." She stared at him. "You really didn't know?"

"But he's so old. He must be thirty!"

"Thirty-one."

"And you . . ."

"Would it be wrong, in your world? But this is your world now. I was betrothed to Marcus when I was twelve. We are to be married in the summer, when I am fourteen."

His world now? He felt stunned. He said, all smiling over: "But . . . do you love him?"

"Of course," Lavinia said. "He is to be my husband."

She put her hand on his arm. "Listen, Simonus. Don't let anyone know I told you this because it's meant to be a surprise. Grandfather has decided to adopt you into our family. Isn't that marvellous? You will be my brother!"

None of the family was stirring when Simon asked the groom to saddle his horse. But the steward, Mandarus, came out as he was preparing to mount.

"You leave early, young master."

"Yes, Mandarus." He paused. "Thank you for all your kindness."

"Will you return soon?"

He shook his head. "Not soon."

Mandarus nodded. His look was sympathetic.

"God go with you."

The others had planned to put in at Dover only long enough to take on provisions and stores. By now they might be preparing to weigh anchor—might already have done so. He cursed himself for his stupidity in not getting away as soon as she had told him; he could have been three hours on his way before nightfall. He urged on the horse, recalling the interminable dinner, sharing a couch with the fatuous Marcus, and watching Lavinia smile at them both from across the table.

The road ran through Canterbury, Durovernum here. He fed and watered his horse and gobbled bread and meat at an inn not far from the town's southern gate. If the fireball should return, he could step through it to see tourists gaping at the broken remnants of the wall, which here was high and solid. But he didn't care about the fireball or what lay beyond it. All that mattered was that it was midafternoon, and he was still more than twenty miles from the port. He threw money to the innkeeper and went running to his horse.

Daylight was fading as he rode into Dover, and his hopes with it. They disappeared completely when he had scanned the quayside. None of the ships tied up was the *Stella Africanus*, but well out in the harbour, putting to sea, was one that might be.

He turned away, feeling sick. Not looking where he was going, he bumped into someone. A voice cursed him, then called his name. He looked up.

"Bos!" He said stupidly: "But there's no ship. I looked for her."

"Just as well you didn't stay a gladiator if that's the quality of your eyesight! A *retiarius* with a broken leg would net you while you were still looking for him. They're short of wharf room, so we had to tie up on the far side of that Spanish wine ship. A mean lot, Spaniards—didn't even offer us a swig."

He felt too dazed to say anything.

"You left it late, lad. We're sailing on the evening tide." Bos grinned down at him. "But at least you've grown up. Come, and I'll take you on board."

XII

THEY HAD TWO WEEKS of reasonably good weather before the storms hit them. The first blew itself out in a couple of days, but the second was more severe and lasted twice as long. Simon was sick in the first, and sicker in the second, but too busy to brood over it. He was left with a confused memory of coldness and wetness and soreness and nausea, but all subordinate to an overpowering weariness.

The second storm had hit them bow on, and for the succeeding four days, without sight of sun or stars, they had no idea where they were being carried through the howling grey waste of water. But they emerged from it still pointed west, and with a fresh southeaster that filled the sails as soon as they were rehoisted. The chickens that had been taken on board at Dubris had been laying unattended, and though some of the eggs were broken, there were enough whole for Brad to cook them ham and eggs—a combination new to Curtius and Bos and greeted with enthusiasm as a specimen of the cuisine of their country-to-be. Simon did not feel hungry when the cooking started, but by the time the meal was ready, nausea had given way to hunger, and he wolfed it down with the rest.

During the last stage of the storm one of the four goats had broken its neck; fortunately not the billy. (Brad had picked the goat as the most useful non-American animal they could take with them.) Bos skinned and butchered it with surprising skill, prepared a stew, and salted the rest of the carcase. They broached a small cask of wine, but it had turned to vinegar from the buffeting. That somewhat dampened the atmosphere of cheerfulness, for Bos especially, but Brad assured them the vine shoots they had also brought would flourish in the rich soil of America; there would be wine enough in years to come.

Simon and Brad were alone on deck that night. Referring to the earlier conversation, Simon said: "You didn't have to keep the same name."

"Of what?"

"America. No Amerigo Vespucci in this world. You could call it anything you like. Bradland."

"With Simon City as its capital? I guess America will do. Not a bad idea to keep some old things when you're making a new beginning."

Overhead the stars, in their familiar constellations, were diamonds on a backcloth of black velvet; the moon was not due to rise for an hour or two. Simon found the Great Bear and traced a path to the polestar. They were still on course, heading west towards the New World, the old one in their wake.

He said: "Do you think new beginnings do any good?"

143

Brad laughed. "Spoken like a true Brit!"

"Look what happened back there. That was a new beginning with a vengeance, wasn't it? We helped overthrow a two-thousand-year-old empire. And the tyranny which existed previously has been replaced by one which could be a whole lot worse."

Brad was silent for a while. Ropes creaked and groaned, and the mainsail cracked in a heavier gust of wind. He said at last: "I wouldn't deny that. There's always a possibility of things turning out bad. But I don't think it's a good reason for not going on trying."

"I suppose you're right." He yawned mightily. "Well, of course you're right."

"Go below," Brad said, "and get some sleep. I'll yell if I want help." He added, as Simon turned to go: "I don't think I got around to thanking you for coming along. I learned during the past few days that three pairs of hands would have been a real case of undermanning. Dangerous, too."

"No thanks due. I was glad to find you at Dover. Very glad."

"What happened—at the villa?"

He had not previously asked questions, and Simon had not felt like volunteering information. He said: "She's going to marry Marcus Cornelius."

"No kidding?" Brad laughed. "Sorry. But look on the bright side, fella. Pocahontas lies ahead."

The days and weeks went by. There was a bad patch when they found the reserve supply of biscuits had been damaged by seawater and were mildewed; it threw both Curtius and Bos into depression. Curtius was morose and spent the whole of his nonworking time huddled silent in his bunk. Bos was more vocally despairing. He talked of the world's edge and the great waterfall that plunged there; when, in a good wind, the ship moved more swiftly, he guessed they were being borne by the current that would sweep them faster and faster to that final drop into eternity. There was no land ahead. After the distance they had travelled, there could be none.

Brad stared into the big man's face.

"There is a land, Bos. A great rich land, greater and richer than anything you could imagine. I was born there. Do you think I am a liar?"

Bos looked back mournfully. "Tell me about it, Bradus. Tell me of your land and its wonders."

Brad told him. He spoke of the great rivers, the mountains higher than those in the land of the Helvetii, the plains in which one might set down the island of Britain six times over and still have room to spare. He spoke of trees that grew more than fifty times the height of a man. And the animals—buffalo and antelope in numbers beyond counting, bears that stood seven feet tall, wolves and mountain lions, succulent prairie chickens and pigeons in flocks that blackened the sky at noon . . .

Even Simon was impressed. Bos said: "If you lie, Bradus, you lie well. It sounds like Elysium, the land of the blessed."

"It is," Brad assured him earnestly. "Exactly that."

Bos shook his head. "But they also say that Elysium is a part of Hades." He sighed deeply. "Well, we have come so far that we might as well go on, even if it does mean sailing over the world's rim."

They had been seven weeks out of sight of land when the really big one hit them. It roared in from the stern quarter, so fast developing that they barely had time to

145

furl the mainsail and the lateens—the bow sail was ripped from its spar before they could get to it. This was in what should have been the hour before dawn, but no dawn came that day. There were a few hours of dismal grey around noon; the rest of the time blackness, lit by the darting fury of lightning. The seas were enormous, lifting the little ship to mountainous peaks and dropping her sickeningly into huge gulfs.

There was nothing to do but stay below and concentrate on bracing oneself against being hurled into a bulkhead. Simon was not sick this time, but was not sure that was an improvement. It made him more aware of what was likely going on around him and what might be going to happen. Increasingly the probabilities were that the next wave would swamp the tiny boat, or else her tortured keel would break and toss them out into the cold dark waters. There came a point when he was almost hoping for it, as an end to the misery.

The storm lasted through the day and night. The following day it eased up slightly, only to renew itself and come on more fiercely. It was three days more before they were able to go on deck and stare at a calm grey sky above a sullenly heaving sea.

The *Stella Africanus* was a mess. The mainmast had survived, but the sternpost which bore the swan had broken off and showed a jagged end. On the port side the hogging planks, which ran from stem to stern, had been completely torn away, and those on the starboard side had been battered in.

"Well," Brad said, "she's not too bad. Leaking a little, but she's still afloat. Neptune had to go without his breakfast, after all."

The joke wasn't funny, but Bos laughed, and after a mo-

146

ment Simon did, too. They were light-headed, from tension and hunger and lack of sleep.

Then Curtius called from the stern: "The rudder doesn't answer. Must have broken her blade."

It stopped the laughter. Brad asked: "Can we rig something up?"

"If we got one of the lateens onto the bow spar," Curtius said, "it would give us some steering. Not much, though."

Simon said: "Maybe we shan't need much."

He pointed across the starboard bow, to where the greys of sea and sky met.

"That smudge on the horizon. Do you think it could be land?"

They camped on a grassy ridge directly above the shore where the *Stella Africanus* lay beached; the breaker which had brought her in had wedged her firmly into the shingle. Another goat had died in the final storm, but again, luckily, it had not been the billy; the three tethered survivors were placidly munching grass. The rooster had been put in a makeshift coop with his hens. Bos had built a primitive oven, using broken planks from the *Stella* as fuel. On this, the morning of the second day, smoke rose straight into a clear blue sky, and the air was sweet with the smell of baking bread. It was very cold, but crisp and invigorating.

The sensation of land underfoot was still strange; Simon found himself swaying as he walked. He and Brad were exploring inland, towards a wood a couple of hundred yards from the beach. Brad was giving reasons why he thought they might have made a landfall somewhere on the coast of New York State. Or maybe Delaware.

He stopped as they both saw them at the same time, standing by the edge of the trees: three figures, bronzed and breech-clouted, with feathers in their tightly bound black hair. Brad said quietly: "Another new beginning?"

Simon muttered: "Any chance of legging it back to the others? We don't even have a knife between us."

Brad stared ahead. "Anywhere along this seaboard," he said, "it's odds-on they're Algonquians."

He walked forward, and after a moment's hesitation Simon followed him. The figures remained motionless. When they were a few feet away, Brad stopped and raised his hands, palms outward. He said something incomprehensible. The figures gazed in silence.

"Wrong word?" Brad said. "Or wrong Indians? Either way . . ."

Suddenly the one in the middle, the tallest of the three, put his own hands up, copying Brad's gesture. He spoke something, more gutturally but plainly an echo of what Brad had said. Brad gave a short whistle of relief.

"What was that?" Simon asked.

"Langundowoágan," Brad said.

Simon looked at him.

"It's Algonquian for *peace.*"